"I'm a screwup—always have been and always will be, I guess."

Sammy said the words bleakly.

"I don't believe that."

"You don't?" He stared at the ground, unwilling to meet her gaze until she drew his attention by lightly clasping his hand.

"No. We all screw up. It doesn't define us unless we let it."

Aubrey squeezed his hand before letting it go. He expelled a short breath and stared out toward the field. "Yeah, well, actions speak louder than words and frankly, I've got people lining up to tell me what a jackass I've been, so what does that say?"

She smiled. "It says people care about you and know you can do better. People rise to the level of our expectations."

"And what did people expect of you?" he asked, turning the tables on her.

Dear Reader,

Harlequin Books is celebrating its 60th year in publishing and I'm so proud to be part of this wonderful family. The first Harlequin book I read was *A Thousand Roses* by Bethany Campbell. I still have it, tucked away in a drawer, and every now and again I take it out and reread it. It's that good.

Being a published author is a dream come true, from working with my wonderful editor, Johanna Raisanen, to seeing my book on the shelves. And it all started with that first Harlequin novel that found itself in my hands so many years ago.

A Man Worth Loving is my seventh novel published by Harlequin—I hope you enjoy Sammy and Aubrey's story. Many readers have asked about Sammy Halvorsen, wondering if he was going to get his own story. Well, here it is. Probably not what was expected, but I think you'll enjoy it.

Hearing from readers is one of my greatest joys (aside from really good chocolate), so don't be shy. Feel free to drop me a line at my Web site, www. kimberlyvanmeter.com, or through snail mail at P.O. Box 2210, Oakdale, CA 95361.

Happy reading,

Kimberly Van Meter

A Man Worth Loving
Kimberly Van Meter

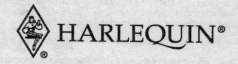

HARLEQUIN®

TORONTO • NEW YORK • LONDON
AMSTERDAM • PARIS • SYDNEY • HAMBURG
STOCKHOLM • ATHENS • TOKYO • MILAN • MADRID
PRAGUE • WARSAW • BUDAPEST • AUCKLAND

Recycling programs
for this product may
not exist in your area.

ISBN-13: 978-0-373-71600-5

A MAN WORTH LOVING

ABOUT THE AUTHOR

An avid reader since before she can remember, Kimberly Van Meter started her writing career at the age of sixteen when she finished her first novel, typing late nights and early mornings on her mother's portable typewriter. Although that first novel was nothing short of literary mud, with each successive piece of work her writing improved, to the point of reaching that coveted published status.

Kimberly, now a journalist, and her husband and three kids make their home in Oakdale, California. She enjoys writing, reading, photography and drinking hot chocolate by the windowsill when it rains.

Books by Kimberly Van Meter

HARLEQUIN SUPERROMANCE

1391—THE TRUTH ABOUT FAMILY
1433—FATHER MATERIAL*
1469—RETURN TO EMMETT'S MILL*
1485—A KISS TO REMEMBER*
1513—AN IMPERFECT MATCH*
1577—KIDS ON THE DOORSTEP*

*Home in Emmett's Mill

Love is a gift we all deserve. This book is dedicated to anyone who's ever had their heart broken in the worst way, yet found the courage to love again.

CHAPTER ONE

THERE WAS A TIME WHEN SOME might've said that
Sammy Halvorsen lived a charmed life, but—as Sammy
cracked his eyelids open and squinted against the harsh
sunlight, the taste of last night's party still on his
tongue—those days were definitely over.

Those days ended exactly six months, sixteen days
and four hours ago.

Dragging a hand across the scruff of his cheeks to
wipe at his mouth, he struggled to a sitting position on
the sofa just in time to hear his front door opening. He
groaned silently. He'd forgotten—or maybe he'd just
blocked it out of his mind—that his mother was coming
with a friend to discuss something he had no interest in
discussing.

"Samuel?" His mother's sharp query clanged in his
head and set off a riot of pain that would gain no
sympathy from Mary Halvorsen simply for the reasons
he was hurting. Tying one on didn't rate on Mary's
Sympathy-O-Meter; neither did anything Sammy was
doing these days. And Sammy didn't have the energy
to argue the fact with her.

"In here," he answered with a scratch in his throat. He cleared it and tried again. "In the living room, Ma."

She appeared in the doorway and the smile on her face froze when she took in his appearance. Deep disappointment or anger—he wasn't really sure but neither boded well for him—flashed in her expression, but he was too hungover to try and charm his way back into her good graces. Everything these days took too much effort. Instead, he ran a hand through his hair and then gestured to the sofa. "Can I get you some coffee or something?" he asked, pulling himself up to walk with an unsteady gait to the small kitchen.

"Coffee would be fine, Samuel," Mary said.

Sammy swayed when he reached for the dark roast blend, grimacing as the world tilted on its axis and he nearly lost whatever was souring his stomach. That would not go over well, he thought with dark humor. "Anything for your friend?" he asked, once he'd finally noticed the petite blonde standing beside his mother.

The woman shook her head and, following Mary's lead, gingerly took a seat on the sofa where previously Sammy had crashed for the night, too drunk to even make it down the short hallway to his bed.

Sammy could hear murmured conversation between the two as he filled the coffeemaker and set it to brew. He wondered why he'd agreed to this meeting. Right now he was just wishing they'd go away so he could return to that blissful sleep of the inebriated. But, as he returned with two full mugs, one for his mom and one for himself, he knew the chances of that happening were slim to none.

This was an intervention Mary Halvorsen–style, and it would take more than his discomfort to sway her from her mission.

"Maybe we should come back another time," the woman suggested, as if reading Sammy's mind. He lifted his mug to her and cracked a grin but it must've come out looking more like a grimace, for she didn't respond favorably. "You don't seem…well."

"He's hungover," Mary said before Sammy could answer, and he frowned. "Too bad for him, I say. I didn't rearrange my schedule to accommodate this meeting just to reschedule because my son doesn't have a lick of sense in his fool head these days." She speared Sammy with a short look as she asked pointedly, "Where's Ian?"

At the mention of his son's name, Sammy took another bracing sip of his coffee and zeroed in on a dust bunny on the floor. "With Annabelle and Dean. I forgot about today. I needed to go out last night."

"What you *need* is a nanny. Someone who can help you take care of Ian. It's not fair to Dean and Annabelle to keep shouldering your responsibility when they have a little one of their own. This has gone on long enough, Samuel."

Sammy couldn't respond to that. He knew she was right, but inside his chest was a useless shell where his heart used to be, and he had nothing left for his young son. It hurt just to look at the kid. If it hadn't been for him, Dana would still be here. Sammy blinked back the wave of shame that followed and finished his coffee in two scalding swallows.

"What's your name?" he asked the woman.

"Aubrey...Aubrey Rose. I just want to say that I'm so sorry for your l—"

"You know much about kids?"

She started at the interruption. "Well, I was an au pair during college and I did a lot of babysitting when I was a kid."

"What the hell is an au pair?"

"It's another word for nanny, used mostly in Europe. I spent a year in Italy.... Anyway, yes, to answer your question I have some experience. I'm also CPR and first aid trained."

"See?" Mary said. "Perfect. More than perfect. And she can start immediately."

Sammy glanced away. Not perfect. Everything was *far* from perfect but who was he to belabor the point? It didn't much matter either way.

He gestured to his mom. "How do you two know each other?"

"We met at the Quilters Brigade," Mary answered. "And before you open your mouth to say some kind of joke, let me spare you the effort. I am not in a joking sort of mood."

"Jeez, Ma, lighten up. You'll scare the young folk," he said, his mouth curving in a tired grin, but he dropped it quickly enough when his mother's stare narrowed. She wasn't kidding. "So the Quilters Brigade…"

Aubrey shrugged. "It's a relaxing hobby and I usually donate the piece when I'm finished."

"Not from around here, I take it?"

"No. I'm a transplant, as Mary calls it."

"Yeah," he said, trying hard not to remember that Dana had been an outsider, too. He swallowed and looked away. "I guess you'll do well enough. Hell, I don't know the first thing about babies so you're already more qualified than me to take care of him." And that fact sliced him to the bone every single day.

AUBREY SHOULD'VE KNOWN this wasn't going to work out. What had she been thinking? She slanted a look at Mary, realizing that the older woman hadn't been entirely honest about her son's situation. This was more than a widower needing help with his infant son. This man was a train wreck. And she wasn't interested in hitching a ride. She had enough baggage to sink the *Titanic*. She didn't need this guy's, as well.

Aubrey gathered her purse, ready to leave when the front door opened and a curvy redhead walked in cradling a bundle against her shoulder. "Sorry, Sammy, but something came up and I had to bring Ian home. I know you said you'd come by later but… *Oh!* I'm interrupting. Mary said you were interviewing a nanny. I'm so sorry. You must be Aubrey?"

Aubrey nodded and the woman continued in a rush,

gently dropping a full diaper bag to the floor and bringing the baby to his father, which by the expression on his face was about as pleasurable as having a nail pounded into his foot. He held the child awkwardly, almost away from his body so as to limit contact, and was quick to hand the child to his grandmother, who immediately started snuggling the boy. "I'm Annabelle," she said. "Nice to meet you. You're going to love Ian. He's the sweetest baby. Mary, I'll see you later?"

"Eight o'clock. Bring Jasmine. I haven't had my granddaughter fix in two days."

"Will do. Oh, one more thing, there are a few pre-prepared bottles in the diaper bag that need to go into the fridge right away. Okay, bye!"

In a blink, Annabelle was gone again but Sammy had hardly registered her presence after she'd put the baby in his arms.

Even as Mary continued to lavish the child with whispered endearments, Aubrey caught a look so full of anguish in Sammy's eyes that for a moment her own heart spasmed. But it was gone in an instant, replaced by that dull, empty stare that said *I care about nothing and no one so don't even try,* and Aubrey knew taking this job would be a mistake.

She opened her mouth with the intent to decline but Mary took that moment to place the baby in her arms. As Aubrey held that soft body she felt an echo of an old pain that never truly healed no matter how many years she put between it and herself. Babies. She loved them.

Truly and deeply. All sorts, all kinds. They were her Achilles' heel. And it was the cruelest of ironies that she would never bear one.

"Aubrey, meet Ian Samuel Halvorsen. Isn't he a doll?"

Aubrey nodded. About that part, Mary hadn't lied. This child was beautiful with a full head of dark hair, porcelain skin and a rosebud mouth that was nearly too pretty for a boy. In fact, if he hadn't been decked out in a sleeper with airplanes on it and gripping a blue blanket it might've been hard to tell his gender. But then again, babies at this age were sometimes hard to tell anyway. She couldn't resist bending down to inhale that sweet intoxicating baby scent and knew even as she did so, walking away was going to be difficult.

"He's beautiful," Aubrey said softly, a slow but reluctant smile forming on her mouth. "Does he look like his mother?"

"The spitting image," Sammy choked out before leaving the room on legs so stiff it looked as if his back might crack from the pressure.

Oh, Lord. That man was drowning. It didn't take a degree in psychology to see that and Aubrey knew from firsthand experience that drowning people often took down the people trying to save them. She hadn't put her life back together only to have it torn apart again by someone else.

Aubrey handed Ian back to his grandmother. "Mary, I like you and I appreciate the opportunity you've offered me but I think this job is more than I can handle."

After a moment, Mary said, "Ian needs you, Aubrey."

"Me? Why me?"

"I'm going to level with you because I get the feeling that you can see right through bullshit and I'm not going to waste your time feeding you any. I'm too old to be raising my grandchild, and my other two sons are busy trying to raise their own families. Annabelle is wearing herself out trying to do everything for Sammy because Dana was her best friend and that's how she deals with her own grief. But Sammy needs to start bonding with his son. He can't do that if he has too many people picking up the slack for him and that's what's been happening since Dana died."

"How is hiring a nanny going to help him with that?"

"It will allow him to break in slowly." Mary inhaled softly as she touched Ian's downy cheek. "He loves his boy. He just doesn't want to right now."

Aubrey shook her head, her gut instinct telling her to stick with her initial decision and decline, but she was secretly horrified at the idea of leaving the baby to his father's emotional void. Babies needed love and affection to grow and thrive. She doubted Samuel Halvorsen was capable of that right now. So where did that leave Ian? *You can't save every child,* a voice warned. No, but she could at least help this child for a short while. No one said she had to get emotionally involved. And no one said she had to stay forever.

"I'll take the job—temporarily. I understand what you're saying about your son needing to break in slowly but if it turns out that I think it's not helping, I'm going to give notice."

"Fair enough." Mary rose and placed the boy in the swing. "I'll go get Sammy so you two can talk salary."

The gently swaying swing drew her attention and she withheld a sigh. She was such a sucker for a sweet face.

Her attention strayed to the photographs on the walls. There were several of Sammy with his late wife. Mary had said her name was Dana and they'd only been married a short time before she died. Aubrey tucked a stray piece of hair behind her ear and couldn't help but feel sad for the young family. A son left without a mother and a husband left without a wife. Sometimes life dealt crappy cards.

Mary returned with Sammy and Aubrey sat a little straighter, projecting as much detached professionalism as she knew how to, and even did a good job of dismissing the casual observations that drifted through her mind as he started talking compensation, schedules and whatnot. Observations such as the dark golden scruff on his face, which was a shade lighter than the tousled mess on top of his head, and the mesmerizing hazel of his eyes that, even bloodshot from a night of tearing up the town, were still pretty arresting. No doubt about it, this guy was a looker. He had that rugged, construction-worker thing going on that would cap off a calendar of hot guys quite nicely, alongside the requisite batch of firefighters and military men. Not her type, really. She could almost hear her mother's voice carping in her ear that Sammy Halvorsen might very well be her type if she were looking to get her heart broken—yet again—but she wasn't so it didn't matter, right?

No, Sammy Halvorsen was so off-limits he might as well be orbiting a separate planet. As far as bad habits went, rehabilitating brokenhearted men was by far her worst. Catching a man on the rebound wasn't something Aubrey wanted to do ever again. No matter how attractive the man was or how adorable his baby was.

Besides, what was she worried about, anyway? It wasn't like she was looking for love—far from it—so everything should be fine.

"When can you start?" he asked abruptly.

Mary interjected with a firm shake of her head before Aubrey could answer. "Not today. She has plans. Tomorrow is soon enough," she added with an arched brow. "You can handle your boy for one night, can't you?"

"Of course I can," he said, but his eyes said something else entirely.

Aubrey checked the frown she felt building in her brow. It was no business of hers what kind of relationship Sammy had with his son. Her job would be to feed, clothe and otherwise care for Ian but no one said anything about getting personally involved.

She cast one final look over her shoulder as she followed Mary out and caught sight of Sammy staring down at his son, gently swaying in the swing, with an expression of—dare she say it?—resentment, and

Aubrey wanted to give Samuel Halvorsen an earful. That man didn't know how to count his blessings.

Stay professional, she admonished herself. This was a job…nothing more.

CHAPTER TWO

SAMMY WINCED AGAINST THE PAIN in his head and, ignoring his son's outstretched hands as he passed the swing, went straight for the kitchen for some aspirin. Ian fussed when it was apparent Sammy wasn't going to liberate him from the swing but Sammy couldn't possibly deal with the kid when his head was about to explode. He washed down three extra-strength pain relievers with a generous swallow of a fresh beer and then leaned against the counter, closing his eyes against Ian's gathering howl. Sammy rubbed at his eyes and then drained the can so he could crush it and leave it behind in the kitchen. So what if it was only 10:00 a.m.? A little hair of the dog was what he was going to need to deal with the screamer in the other room.

Ian's face was red and scrunched from crying, his big, round eyes staring at Sammy reproachfully as he lifted his chubby arms again, whimpering until Sammy pulled him free to put him on the floor. But that's not what Ian wanted, either, apparently because he wiggled and kicked and screamed until Sammy was quite sure the kid was going to have a heart attack or something. Alarmed, he picked him up and gently but awkwardly jostled him the way he'd seen Annabelle do with Ian and her daughter Jasmine when they fussed. It seemed to work for a minute but before Sammy could enjoy the reprieve, the kid yowled loud enough to bring the house down.

"Damn, kid, what's your problem?" he muttered, jostling him a little less gently, which only made it worse. "Are you hungry or something?" he asked. He tilted his son upside down so he could sniff his drawers. He drew back quickly. "Oh, gross. Dude? Seriously! We're going to have to work on that. That's disgusting."

His alcohol-soaked brain wasn't functioning on higher levels, and for a second he couldn't remember how to change a diaper. His gaze sought and found the diaper bag Annabelle had dropped off, and he grabbed it. With one hand holding Ian in a football pose, which the kid didn't like one bit, Sammy wrestled with the bag until the contents spilled out, including several bottles, which rolled out and went everywhere. He picked a diaper and the wipes from the pile and proceeded to the sofa.

Ian, near hysterical, waved his hands and kicked his feet so hard Sammy had a hard time grabbing the flailing little suckers so he could take the offending diaper off. "Will you cut it out already? Do you want this thing off or not?" he demanded and Ian squeezed more tears down his cheeks, which made Sammy feel ten times worse for being so rough with him. "Sorry, kid…." he muttered, but he was too busy trying to wipe the crap—holy hell, how'd a kid so small make such a mess?—from Ian's little bare butt to waste time on apologies that the baby wouldn't understand anyway. His brother Dean had tried to tell him that the tone of his voice was important when dealing with kids, especially when they're young, but honestly, Sammy hadn't been interested in taking parenting classes with his wife fresh in the grave.

Finally, he got Ian clean and into a fresh outfit, because the one he'd been in now had baby poop all over it, but Ian was still puckering his face, getting ready to wail. "C'mon, help a guy out. What's wrong?" he moaned, collapsing against the back of the sofa and staring at the ceiling in misery. Suddenly, Ian slid from the sofa, startling Sammy, to land on the floor with an *oof* that knocked the wind out of the little guy so it took a moment for the real screaming to start.

"Oh, God, are you okay?" he exclaimed, rushing to pick up his son, scared that the kid was truly hurt. When Ian didn't stop screaming, he did the only thing he knew how to do in this kind of situation. He called Annabelle.

AUBREY WAS IN THE QUILTING shop, perusing new fabrics, when she overheard Mary talking with her daughter-in-law Annabelle. Aubrey didn't mean to eavesdrop but her ears perked when she heard they were talking about Ian.

"He's fine," Annabelle assured Mary, who wore a concerned frown on her face. "He just got the wind knocked out of him, but I told Sammy he should never leave Ian on the sofa without watching him. He's just learning to roll over on his own. The sofa's not that high off the ground but if it'd been the bed...he might've been really hurt."

Mary scowled. "That boy ought to be horsewhipped for the idiot he's being. I don't know what's gotten into him. He was raised better than that, I can tell you that right now. His father and I are beside ourselves...." Mary stopped as Aubrey approached, her tirade momentarily halted. A bright smile followed. "Why, Aubrey, hello, I didn't see you there. You remember my daughter-in-law Annabelle?"

"Nice to see you again," Aubrey murmured, taking in the beautiful, curvy redhead and the little blond girl skipping around her feet. She smiled at the girl, who had stopped to stare at her with wide, inquisitive blue eyes. "Is this your daughter?" she asked Annabelle.

"One of them. This is Honey. My baby, Jasmine, is home with her dad. I just needed to talk with Mary about Ian. I knew she'd be here at the shop so I made a quick stop. You're going to be Ian's nanny, I hear?"

"Yes. I start this afternoon. What happened to Ian? I couldn't help but overhear."

"Oh, it was nothing really but it shook Ian up a little. He took a tumble off the sofa and it knocked the wind out of him. He was totally fine when he got some love and affection. And a bottle. Poor guy was starving. I told Sammy I left him some preprepared bottles in the diaper bag but I found them under the sofa."

"What kind of formula does he use?" Aubrey asked, getting a notepad ready to jot down the brand. Mary and Annabelle exchanged a look and Aubrey wondered what she'd inadvertently said wrong.

"He doesn't drink formula much," Annabelle said, pausing. "Depending on your philosophies, this may sound really strange, but I express breast milk for Ian."

"Excuse me?" Aubrey started, not quite sure she heard that correctly. "Did you say you're breast-feeding your nephew?"

"No, I said I'm expressing breast milk for my nephew."

Mary intervened, speaking warmly of her daughter-in-law as she explained. "You see, Dana died in childbirth. A rarity in this day and age but it still happens. Annabelle had only just given birth to Jasmine a month earlier and because Dana had planned to breast-feed for as long as possible, Annabelle started expressing milk for Ian before he even left the hospital because she knew it was what Dana would've wanted."

Aubrey didn't know how to respond. The concept was so foreign to her. Her own mother hadn't breast-fed, saying it wasn't seemly to be seen with two babies hanging off her chest as if she was some kind of baboon in the jungle. Annabelle mistook Aubrey's silence for reproach and stiffened. "It's perfectly natural. Back in the medieval days, royalty often used a wet nurse. It's healthier than formula and helps with their immune system."

Aubrey wasn't judging, though it was certainly a

shock. Aubrey tried to imagine what her mother would have to say about that and nearly giggled at how appalled Barbie would be. Her twin sister, Arianna, would likely mirror that horror. They'd both arch perfectly waxed eyebrows in distaste and remark on how white trash it all was. "I think it's beautiful that you loved your friend so much you would do that for her son," Aubrey said.

Annabelle's eyes watered for a brief moment. "Thank you. I just want the best for him. She wanted a baby so badly. When she got pregnant we cried together. I think she told me before she told Sammy. It was the happiest moment of her life."

"How'd Samuel react to the news?" Aubrey inquired, not quite comfortable using her employer's more familiar nickname.

"He was happy but I think he would've given Dana the moon if she asked for it even if he preferred sunlight. Dana was the one who really wanted to start a family right away and it took a while to get pregnant. Dana called Ian her miracle baby."

Aubrey's eyes threatened to water, wishing there'd been such a miracle in her own life. *Don't go there.* She forced a bright smile. "It was nice to meet you. I suppose I'll see you two a lot while I'm Ian's nanny. I hope to become good friends."

And then, before either could say anything further, she left the shop.

It wasn't until she was halfway to her rented house

that she realized she'd forgotten all about the quilting fabric she'd wanted to check out. She sighed heavily and put it out of her head. She needed to get ready for her first day of work.

SAMMY SLAPPED A LITTLE aftershave on his cheeks and winced when tiny nicks from the quick shave job screamed at the alcohol splash. He sucked in a breath and then grinned in the mirror, his best roguish charmer that usually worked pretty well on the ladies, and then, remembering that his jeans were still in the dryer, he stepped out of his bedroom to find Aubrey in the hallway. She seemed frozen to the spot, a look of chagrin and embarrassment on her face.

She turned quickly and stammered an apology. "The door was open.... I didn't realize... I thought you said to be here... Oh, I'm a few minutes early, though, not because I'm one of those people who are ridiculously punctual, well, actually, I am one of those people because I hate to be late—"

"It's okay," he said gruffly to her rambling. If he hadn't been embarrassed himself, he might've found the humor in the situation, but at the moment he wasn't feeling anything but intense mortification at being caught with nothing but a towel around his ass on his nanny's first day on the job. *Nice going.* If she didn't quit right then and there it'd be a miracle. He wrapped the towel a bit tighter to ensure there weren't any wardrobe malfunctions and said to her back, "Kid's asleep in his swing.

Why don't you go wait in there while I get dressed." She bobbed her head in agreement before skittering away.

He detoured to the dryer and jerked the jeans up over his hips quickly. When he was decent, he sent a prayer to heaven that she was still willing to take the job and tried that charming smile on again to up the odds of her staying.

She rose from the sofa where she'd been fidgeting with the strap of her purse when he entered the living room. He waved away her attempts to apologize again. "It's my fault. I'm not quite used to having someone else in the house and I forgot to grab my clothes before I hit the shower," he said, cringing at the red blush staining her cheeks. "It's okay. Really. No big deal. No harm no foul as they say."

"I'm assuming there will be no more of these types of incidents while I'm in your employ?" she said, her tone implying that perhaps he'd engineered the whole situation.

"Of course not," he said, slightly insulted that the sight of his *toweled* body had offended her so much. There was no reason to make a federal case out of it. "It was an accident. The last thing I need is my kid's nanny to be thinking about me naked," he muttered.

"Not a problem," she retorted, a bit sharply. "I've already put the incident out of my mind."

If it weren't for the high color in her cheeks he might've believed her. But she was holding to it so that was fine with him. He wasn't lying when he said he didn't want the nanny to think of him in any way that wasn't completely professional.

"Good. Now that that's settled…" He rubbed his hands together, ready to move on. He had a date with a longneck bottle, which would hopefully end with a date with a redhead or a blonde…whichever was ready and available. "So, I probably won't be home until late… well, depending on how well things go tonight…"

"How late?" she asked, her brow furrowing a little.

"Uh, well, not sure. Is that a problem? I thought I told you that you might need to be available for overnighters."

"Yes. You did mention the possibility but I didn't realize it would start with my first day. I didn't bring the proper supplies."

He frowned. That certainly put a crimp in his plans. Suddenly he felt as if he had a curfew. He glanced around and his gaze alighted on the kid's car seat in the corner where Annabelle had left it the last time she'd dropped him off. "Here…how about this…if it gets too late you can just take the kid to your place and I'll pick him up later."

Problem solved. Except the disapproving stare coming from his new nanny told him what she thought of that idea. "Oh, never mind. I'll be home before eleven. That work for you?" he bit out, hating that he was giving in. He could tell right now this arrangement wasn't going to work out. He didn't care if his mom picked her out or not. She didn't have to deal with her.

"Thank you," she said, her eyes registering cool victory. "I appreciate your consideration. I don't know the roads around here quite yet and don't feel comfortable driving too late at night."

Yeah, yeah…he wanted to grumble but he didn't. He was just itching to get out of there. He was headed out of town tonight and now his prowl-time just got cut in half. Not even he could close the deal with this short of a window. But he could try. "You have my cell. If there's an emergency…just leave me a voice mail I guess and then call Annabelle. She's real good with stuff like that. She's my brother's wife."

"I've met Annabelle," she interjected.

"Oh? When?" he asked, to be polite. He couldn't really care less and time was ticking. He pocketed his wallet in his back pocket and grabbed his keys.

"Well, don't you remember, she was the one who dropped off Ian yesterday. We met officially this morning in the quilting shop. She was telling me how Ian rolled off the sofa yesterday," she said, although her tone was professional, he sensed her disapproval and he stiffened.

"He was fine," he said.

"Yes, Annabelle told me. I'm glad. Falls can be very serious for a baby Ian's age."

Sammy shifted, annoyed at her prim censure. "Yeah, well, he's fine," he said, moving to the door. "Later."

"Goodbye, Mr. Halvorsen."

He stopped. "Call me Sammy," he said but she shook her head.

"I'd prefer not. You're my employer."

"Oh. Yeah, okay. I guess you're right. But it's just that when you call me Mr. Halvorsen I feel like I should be looking for my dad or something. Plus, it makes me feel old."

She smiled at that but held firm. He felt a scowl coming on but really what did he care what she called him? If she wanted to be all stiff and proper who was he to say she couldn't be? He shrugged. "Suit yourself. Good night, *Ms. Rose*."

AUBREY WATCHED AS SAMMY WALKED out the door, her temper building as she replayed the last five minutes of their conversation through her head. What a self-absorbed jerk. She tried to be understanding because he was a widower and all but he had some nerve to try and come on to her like that. Who wandered around their house in just a towel? Especially when their nanny was supposed to arrive within minutes? And then to try and make her feel as if she was overreacting to his display? Her fists clenched as another wave of anger rolled over her. How did she get herself into this one?

Egad. The ego on that guy. Unfortunately, he probably had plenty of women who were happy to feed that monstrous ego. If she were the brainless type, she could totally see how the man likely charmed his way into countless beds. A smile here, a little flattery, and boom, panties dropped. Her lip curled in open disgust. It was likely he had good qualities somewhere deep—very deep—down, but at the moment, Aubrey couldn't imagine what they could be.

Well, if she were held under a hot bulb in a torture

chamber with someone threatening to pull her finger-nails off she might be forced to admit that he had one helluva physique. He looked damn near carved from stone, like the marble statues at Versailles, except he didn't sport a Roman nose nor was he missing a limb. She inhaled sharply at the traitorous musings and shut them down immediately. *Jerk.* He hadn't even said goodbye to his baby. What kind of father was he?

A terrible one.

She felt a twinge for judging him so quickly, but really, he hadn't made much of a case for himself with that attitude of his. And what kind of person tells a virtual stranger that she can just pack up his child like luggage and take the baby home because it inconveni-ences his party time? *Argggh!* She cored an apple with particular vehemence and nearly sliced through to her hand. She took a deep breath and steadied herself. No point in getting so worked up over one silly, self-absorbed idiot who didn't know how lucky he was.

She looked sorrowfully at the sleeping boy and her heart melted a bit more for the sad circumstances then she went to prepare some food for the little guy. She'd brought her food processor so she could make home-made baby food. He was old enough to start with a few solids but she wanted to start slow so that she didn't inadvertently spark a food allergy in the boy.

Without Sammy in the way, bothering her with his smarmy smiles and perfect body, she started to feel more at ease. The house was small and rustic but there was a coziness to it that appealed to her. It didn't take a rocket scientist to figure that one out. Her mother had ridiculously bourgeois taste that ran toward the faux gold furnishings and lavish tapestries that carpeted the cavernous hallways of the homes she decorated and Aubrey had always found them embarrassingly ostentatious. Yep, Sammy's house was so far from anything Aubrey had ever called home that it was immediately wonderful in Aubrey's opinion.

Humming a wordless tune, she went to work mashing some bananas she'd brought with her and set to boiling water for the apples. Nikki and Violet had loved her homemade applesauce. She frowned slightly as the thought of them still hit a sore spot and started coring more apples. Apparently eight months wasn't enough time to lessen the pain of not having them in her life but she'd loved them so deeply. Her gaze drifted to Ian, who was starting to awaken and sighed heavily. She couldn't let her heart get attached to this one. One corner of her mouth twisted ruefully. At least she didn't have to worry about falling for her employer with this job. Sammy Halvorsen was the last person she'd ever be attracted to.

Thank goodness for small favors.

CHAPTER THREE

SAMMY WAS SHIT-FACED. The woman who was propping him up giggled as he tried to fit his key into the lock and she had to help guide it in.

He made a sexually suggestive comment that made her giggle again and they both fell into the door, slamming it open against the wall.

"Oops." The woman laughed as they stumbled inside, making a racket loud enough to wake the dead. He pressed against her, slanting his mouth over hers, eager to get the party started. Sammy remembered he already had company just as Aubrey came around the corner with a disgusted expression on her face.

His date quickly sobered and looked askance at Aubrey, who appeared the part of a very annoyed housemate, which if Sammy hadn't been two sheets to the wind, he might've realized wasn't funny at all. But as it was, the pinched look on her face was quite comical. "Who is that?" the woman—Sharlene? Sherry? Crap, he couldn't remember—didn't sound amused, either. She turned to him as he used the wall to steady himself.

"I thought you said you weren't married," she said with a definite edge to her voice.

"I'm not." He pushed off from the wall and walked unsteadily toward Aubrey, who looked ready to kick him in the shins with her tiny feet. Boy, she was petite. So different from Dana. Dana had been tall and beautiful, his Amazon wife, he used to tease. Frowning, he gestured toward Aubrey as he walked past her toward the kitchen. "She's my nanny. Want a beer?" he asked.

"Mr. Halvorsen...a moment, please," came Aubrey's firm request as she turned on her heel and marched from the living room. Judging by the way she didn't wait to see if he would comply, she clearly expected him to follow.

Sammy sighed and gestured to the blonde to make herself comfortable while he took care of the situation at hand. He found Aubrey in his bedroom, which suddenly made him intensely uncomfortable. Aubrey in his bedroom was...not right. At all.

As if reading his mind, she peered up at him, tight-lipped and angry. "It's a small house, Mr. Halvorsen. I did not feel it prudent to air my concerns in front of your friend, and I'm not about to wake Ian up by taking this conversation into his room, though by the way you crashed about like a drunken ox it's a wonder the baby didn't wake up screaming," she muttered with a glare.

"We weren't that loud," he said defensively, though he knew that she was probably right. Damn. This nanny rode him harder than his ma, which was probably why Mary Halvorsen hand-selected her.

"You're drunk," she accused, clearly unamused.

"Of course I am," he said, smiling lopsidedly at her. "That's the whole point, ain't it? Have fun, cut up, cut loose—"

"Bring home floozies with your infant son sleeping in the other room," she interrupted and he jerked.

"That's a shitty thing to say."

"Yes. And equally bad because it's true, isn't it?" she queried him, crossing her arms. "Mr. Halvorsen…if this is your type of behavior, the kind of thing I can come to expect from you…"

"Will you stop with the *Mister* already? I told you—"

"And I told you no. The problem I see with you, Mr. Halvorsen, is that you're not accustomed to responsibility. I am your son's nanny. Not yours. You've put me in a pickle, Mr. Halvorsen."

His alcohol-soaked brain zeroed in on the word *pickle* and he chuckled. Who talked like that? It was cute in an annoyingly stuck-up way. If he were attracted to the librarian type, which he wasn't, he might be seriously turned on by her prim and proper routine. But as evidenced by the bleached blonde getting bored and *sober* in his living room…nope, it wasn't the brainy types that turned his head. Although…

She snapped two fingers in front of his face, and he refocused on her. "As I was saying, you've put me in a bad spot. I don't feel comfortable leaving you with Ian in your condition or with the *company* you've chosen to bring home with you—" she might as well have said vermin the way she phrased it "—but I don't feel it's appropriate for me to take Ian out of bed at this late hour and take him home with me. So you leave me no choice but to insist that you send that *woman* home and put yourself to bed."

He balked. "That wouldn't be right. I invited her to stay."

She gave him a steely glare. "Nothing about this situation is right by my estimation. Send her home or I quit."

He cocked a rogue grin her way, oddly charmed by the show of spirit flashing in her eyes. Funny, he hadn't noticed how cute she was. He moved closer and she took a healthy step back. He frowned, stung by her obvious rejection. Now *that* was different. "So quit," he said with a shrug, anger at being rejected coupled with the tequila shots he'd downed earlier combining to make his mouth say really bad things. "It's not like it takes a bunch of skill to watch a kid. I can find another nanny…one who's not so uptight and bitchy."

Her gaze turned wintry and she pushed past him. "Good luck with that, you arrogant jerk," she muttered, moving by him so quickly he stumbled on unsteady feet. "You don't deserve that beautiful boy. It's probably a good thing your wife is dead. If she could see how you're treating the child she died to give life…" She shook her head in disgust as she added, "So pathetic."

And then stomped out the door.

ANGER VIBRATED HER ENTIRE BODY as she got to her car, intent on leaving as quickly as she could, but somehow Sammy managed to get those wobbly drunken muscles to work and he was running after her.

"Wait!" he called out. She tried to ignore him but there was a thread of desperation weaving its way through his tone that made her pause, if only momentarily. He reached the car and skidded to a stop. "I'm sorry…I shouldn't have said that… I've had too much to drink and my mouth got away from me."

"And?"

"And it was completely out of line for me to bring someone home with you still at the house. I wasn't thinking," he admitted, dropping his stare to the ground as if ashamed. She wasn't sure if it was an act or not. She didn't know him well enough to tell but she was suspicious on principle simply by his behavior so far.

She wanted him to admit that it was also bad judgment on his part to bring strangers into the house with an infant but she sensed she wouldn't get that from him. Not yet, anyway.

"Fine," she said tersely. "But your friend needs to leave. Now."

"She's not a bad gal," he started to say but she cut him off with a glare. "Right. Gimme a minute."

Aubrey moved past him, accidentally brushing him with her shoulder. The warmth of his skin through his shirt reminded her that it'd been a long time since she'd enjoyed the comfort of a man's arms. Thankfully, there were no sparks that ignited at the incidental touch. She shuddered at the thought. She didn't pause to offer any words of explanation to the woman sitting forlornly on the sofa and went to check on Ian while Sammy sent her on her way.

Treading softly into Ian's room, her anger melted at the sight of the sleeping boy, so sweet in repose that her heart ached. Why did she have such a tender spot for children? Her life would've been so much easier if she'd been built more like her mother and sister. Arianna, although her twin, couldn't be more her opposite. The idea of caring for a child, even her own, didn't appeal in the least. It was a wonder Barbie had agreed to conceive. Aubrey could only imagine her mother's dismay when she'd learned she was carrying not one, but two babies. She sighed softly and smoothed a lock of dark hair from the boy's soft baby brow. If she were given the gift of motherhood…she'd never squander it.

IT WAS LONG AFTER HE'D regretfully sent Sherry on her way with an effusive promise to call her tomorrow and Aubrey had fallen asleep in his recliner in the living room that Sammy sank into a dark place that was often his resting stop after a long night. Usually he woke with a busty woman at his side and he had to sneak from her house before she woke. He rarely brought his dates home; the thought of letting another woman into his own bed made him shudder with shame. Yet tonight he'd been ready to screw that blonde in the bed he'd shared with Dana. Aubrey had hit the nail on the head when she'd called him pathetic.

He supposed he should thank his nosy and intrusive nanny for keeping him from making yet another huge mistake, but it rankled him that he gave in so easily. She treated him like he was lower than dirt—the looks she gave him could wither a flower on the vine—and yet, she seemed protective of Ian in a way that baffled him. She didn't know the kid, not really. He was the kid's father and he couldn't muster up the appropriate feelings. Scrubbing his hands down his face as if he could wipe away all the guilt that weighed him down, he fell back on his bed, not caring that he was still dressed, nor that he was still wearing his boots. Honestly, what was there to care about any longer?

Dana...why'd you leave me? I'm so lost....

That mournful feeling followed him into sleep, filling the landscape of his dreams with sadness and pain, a vision of Dana dying on that table, giving her last breath as Ian gasped his first.

A tear leaked down Sammy's face and stained his pillow.

"Dana..."

CHAPTER FOUR

SAMMY SHOWED UP ON THE JOB SITE surly and nursing an aching head, and certainly in no mood to deal with either of his older brothers when Dean barked at him.

"You're late," he said.

"Glad to see you can tell time," Sammy grumbled as he buckled his tool belt into place. "I overslept."

Both his brothers exchanged a knowing look and Sammy wanted to put his fist through both of their mugs. "How's the new nanny working out?" Josh asked.

"Fine." If you don't mind the idea of being mothered by a woman who made you feel ten inches tall one minute and oddly turned on in the next. Yeah…it's great. "She's good with the kid," he admitted, hefting a large cement bag onto his shoulder with a grunt. "That's all that matters, right?"

He considered the strange twist of being attracted to her. Frankly, he was hot for anything in a skirt these days but his tastes were pretty predictable. In the old days, before Dana, the thrill of the chase was what got his motor running. Then he met Dana and everything he ever thought he knew about women went right down the toilet. Dana had been cool and distant at first but once he cracked that nut…she'd been fiery and passionate, a woman who could match his appetite bite for bite. An ache so sharp it made him suck in a wild breath almost caused him to drop his load but he recovered before either of his keen-eyed brothers—who continually regarded him like he was on a suicide watch or something—could catch it.

"You gonna stand there gawking at me like a bunch of girls or get to work?" he asked, annoyed when neither seemed inclined to return to their tasks. He dropped the cement bag and went to get another one. "You're giving me the willies staring at me like that."

It was Josh who spoke first. "We're worried about you," he said matter-of-factly.

"You're screwing up. And the way you treat Ian…" At Sammy's scowl, Dean paused but then revved up again. "Annabelle is upset and if Annabelle's upset then you'd better believe that I'm going to get involved."

"Butt out," Sammy warned, trying to walk away, but Dean grabbed him by the shirt and jerked him around to face him. Sammy eyed his brother and practically dared him to push the issue. "Watch it, Dean. The days where you can grab me like a snot-nosed kid are over. I'll lay you out if you grab me again."

Dean grinned. "Go ahead and try, Sammy. Might be the best thing for you to get your stupid head knocked around."

Josh intervened. "Knock if off, both of you. Ma sees either of you with black eyes she's going to give us all matching ones. Listen, Sam, we're your brothers...we just don't want to see you make a mistake you can't take back."

Sammy shrugged off Dean's grip and bent down to grab another cement bag. He hefted it with a grunt. "Don't worry about me. You've got your own lives to worry about. Wives...babies...surely that's enough to keep you out of my business."

"It would be if you'd stop tomcatting around every honky-tonk bar from here to Coldwater. What's gotten into you?" Dean asked, the disgust in his tone mirroring what Sammy had heard in Aubrey's voice last night.

A pang of anguish reminding him just how screwed up he was made him grin like a jackal as he answered, "I'm grieving. Can't you tell?"

Dean's face darkened and Sammy knew he'd gone too far. He half hoped Dean would lay him out. He certainly deserved it. "You sure as hell don't look like you're grieving to me. How do you think it makes Annabelle feel to hear around town about all the women you're nailing like the end of the world is around the corner when her best friend—your supposed *beloved* wife—died just six months ago? It's killing her! The other day she burst into tears because of some story she heard about you and some former coworker of Dana's getting it on outside the bar, in the damned alley! What is wrong with you!"

"Tell your wife to mind her own business," Sammy said and turned to walk away.

And *that* was the final straw. But it wasn't Dean who threw the punch.

It was Josh.

Sammy hit the ground and went into blissful oblivion.

AUBREY BUNDLED IAN UP AGAINST the chill so the boy could have some outside play time before it got too cold to enjoy the fall season. Walking the perimeter of the property, she drew a deep breath of the crisp air and smiled at the rustic beauty of the area, such a stark contrast from where she grew up. Here there were rolling hills of trees and brush, not a manicured lawn in sight, but it took her breath away. So gorgeous. She could imagine Ian running free, weaving in and out of the trees, playing cops and robbers, jumping in mud puddles, and ending the day covered head to toe in dirt. A warm smile followed. How awesome. Then she sighed. "Perhaps if fate hadn't been so cruel as to take your mama and leave you with that self-absorbed man you know as your father, I'd say you were a lucky boy. But sometimes fate is cruel, sweet baby. That is something you may very well learn when you get older," she murmured to Ian, whose cheeks had pinked to a rosy hue and his delighted smile seemed to say that he agreed with her. Impulsively, she bent down and pressed a quick kiss on his crown. *Oh, you shouldn't have done that,* a voice warned inside her head, but she immediately pushed it aside, even though the advice was sound. But babies need love and affection, she protested. It wasn't like the boy's father was going to provide it. She rounded the back side of the house and gasped with pleasure when she saw the young apple tree, bursting with fresh apples, some of which had dropped to the ground to rot.

"Why didn't you tell me you had an apple tree growing in your backyard?" she asked Ian playfully as he watched her with happy eyes. "I'll bet your mom planted this tree when she and your dad got married."

She moved closer and noted the variety of the tree was written on a small tag. "A self-pollinating Gala," she read. She didn't know much about apple trees but she was open to learning. Somehow she knew keeping this tree alive and blooming for the future would've been important to Dana. Plucking an apple, she took an exploratory bite. Juice dribbled down her chin and the crisp flavor was like manna from heaven. "Ohh, this is good," she said. Then looked again to Ian, an idea forming in her mind. "I'll bet your mom has a basket or a bucket we can find that she used to pick these apples. Let's find it."

Just as she figured, Aubrey was able to find a large basket in the laundry room, tucked into the far reaches of the cabinet above the washing machine. She brushed it out, then she and Ian headed back outside to ease the burden of that beautiful apple tree.

SAMMY WAS STILL IN A PISSY mood when he got home, in spite of stopping by the bar first for a beer. His jaw ached where Josh had clocked him and a bruise was beginning to shadow the stubble on his chin. He wasn't sure which was worse—the fact that he'd deserved that punch or the low to which he'd sunk in his mind. It was as if he was in a downward spiral he couldn't do anything to stop and everyone around him was trying to help but he was gunning for that fateful moment when he went *splat* against the concrete. If Dana were here she'd no doubt tell him to quit feeling sorry for himself. A sad smile lifted his mouth, but only for a moment. He couldn't think of Dana. Maybe if Ian didn't look so much like her....

He opened the door and was hit with the savory aroma of something he hadn't smelled in a long time. Apple pie.

Entering the kitchen, the smell triggered a memory that nearly sent him to his knees. He slowed, let his eyes close and sank into the past.

Suddenly, it was September of last year, and Sammy had come home to that same tantalizing aroma.

"Damn, girl, what is that amazing smell?" he'd said, whipping his ball cap off and tossing it to the hat stand by the door. He saw Dana in the kitchen, pregnant, flour in her hair, the room looking as if a bomb had gone off, there was sweat dampening her forehead and one perfect apple pie cooling on the counter. He'd never been so conflicted by his desire to eat pie and make love to his wife. In the end, he did both. Right there on the kitchen floor.

"I thought you might like a pie made from our very own apple tree," she'd said huskily, her voice retaining the warmth created by their lovemaking. She propped herself up on her elbow and stared down at him as he lay on his back recuperating. "I had no idea pie has this kind of effect on you," she teased, her brown hair falling forward to tickle his face.

"*You* have this kind of effect on me," he murmured, pulling her down to his mouth, savoring everything about his wife. "But I do love pie," he added playfully.

"I love you," she said softly.

The echo of Dana's whispered sentiment brought him crashing back to the present, and he found Aubrey staring at him, an uncertain expression on her face.

"What are you doing?" he asked in a strangled tone.

"I...took Ian for a walk and discovered the apple tree...and they were just dropping on the ground," she said, faltering. "I didn't think you would mind if I put them to good use."

"Well, I do mind," he said, shaking with pain. He had a vision of grabbing the ax and chopping the damn tree down so he never had to deal with this happening ever again. But then he noticed that she'd been very busy while he'd been at work. Not only had she baked a pie but she'd made applesauce for Ian and that's what she'd been doing when he walked in, putting the sauce into small containers for later use. He choked down the angry words that bubbled to the surface as he remembered Dana talking about how she'd hoped to do that very thing for their child. She'd been so excited to be a mother, she wanted nothing but the best for the baby—and apparently the best had included homemade applesauce.

Aubrey stiffened and her mouth tightened as she offered a terse apology. "I had no idea you felt so strongly about letting the apples go to waste. I won't do it again," she said.

"Forget it," he bit out, hating the gruff quality of his voice. "I…" He tried to apologize but he couldn't get the words out. Instead, he just turned on his heel and headed to the shower. She was his employee. He didn't owe her explanations.

TEARS STUNG AUBREY'S EYES but she managed to hold them back until Sammy stalked from the room. It was ridiculous, she thought, wiping at her eyes with the back of her hand before returning to her task. Did he have to be such an ass? She twisted a lid onto the last container and stuck it in the freezer with the rest she'd made. She wiped down the counter and put everything in its place then prepared Ian for his bath.

She took great care to avoid looking in the direction of Sammy's bedroom, but she couldn't help wondering what had caused him to snap like that. She didn't want to but she saw the pain in his eyes, and it softened her just a little toward him. *Oh, stop that. He's not a stray, injured dog you can nurse back to health. He's a grown man acting like a spoiled, selfish child. Steer clear.* Odd, how that scolding came straight at her in the voice of her mother. She rolled her eyes at herself and repressed a grateful shudder that the voice was only in her head and not being delivered in person.

After a quick bath and a bottle of milk, Aubrey put Ian to bed. As soon as Ian's eyes drifted shut, she went to Sammy's bedroom and gave the door a soft knock.

"Mr. Halvorsen…I'm taking off. Ian—" She was startled when the door opened abruptly and Sammy stood there, his eyes red-rimmed and his expression stark. She straightened and continued. "As I was saying, Ian has had his bath and his dinner. He's asleep in his bed. Is there anything else you need before I leave?"

He shook his head and she turned. His voice at her back made her stop.

"I'm sorry for…snapping at you," he said quietly.

She nodded, but the motion was stiff. Still, since he was extending an olive branch of sorts, she'd do the same. "I apologize for not asking first. I realize it was presumptuous of me to assume you wouldn't mind if I put the apples to use."

"Does he like the applesauce you made for him?" he asked.

"He does. Very much."

He ran his tongue across his lip and it was then Aubrey noticed the swelling along his jaw.

"What happened to you?" she asked, appalled at the injury and his apparent disregard for his own care. "Come here," she instructed, forgetting for the moment that she thought he was the lowest of all men who hardly deserved more than a cursory glance much less her help. She led him to the kitchen where the light was better and then set about putting together an ice pack. "Was this a fight?"

"Something like that," he answered with a shrug.

"Kiss the wrong girl? One with a husband perhaps?" she muttered and he chuckled darkly as he accepted the ice pack and set it against his jaw.

"Nothing like that. My brother wanted to teach me some manners."

"Your own brother did this?" she repeated, horrified.

"Yeah." He paused, then added, "I said something I shouldn't have."

"So you deserved it?"

He lifted the ice pack. "Josh wouldn't have done it if he didn't feel it was justified. Now, if it'd been Dean…he has more of a temper. And he's been known to swing a few punches here and there. Just ask Aaron Eagle. He's felt the sting of my brother's fist. But he had it coming, too."

"Who is Aaron Eagle?" she asked.

Sammy tried to grin but the effort cost him and he winced instead. He waved away her question. "Nobody. Just a guy my brother Dean doesn't much care for. Dean clocked Aaron one day at a construction site. But trust me, the guy had it coming."

"Sounds like your brothers are a couple of violent ruffians," Aubrey observed, not quite sure what to think of this information. She only knew Dean by association through Annabelle and Mary and it was hard to reconcile this image of the eldest Halvorsen brother with what she was hearing.

"Are you still fighting with your brothers?" she asked

cautiously. She didn't mean to pry—it certainly fell under the category of *none of her business*—but she was curious.

"Probably," came his bleak answer. He studied the ice pack in his hand, turning it slowly. He looked at her. "You got brothers or sisters?" he asked.

Startled by his question, she only stared for a moment. He mistook her hesitation and waved away her need to answer but for some reason she wanted to. "I have a twin sister," she said.

He eyed her. "Someone who looks just like you or the other kind?"

"Someone who looks just like me," she said, then added with a fierce glower, "but we're nothing alike. She's more like our mother. I take after my father."

"Where are you from?"

How to answer... She supposed she was from Manhattan but really, her family had houses all over the place. They'd wintered in Manhattan, summered in the Hamptons, it was all so cliché. Her mother had made sure the Rose family was always in the right social circles, attended the right parties, dressed to impress. The whole shallow, superficial nonsense made Aubrey want to gag. Noting Sammy's expectant expression, she made something up. "Vermont."

Why she said Vermont she hadn't a clue but for some reason she couldn't just admit that she'd grown up a privileged nomad, living mostly in hotel penthouses and the occasional sumptuous cottage. Vermont sounded rustic and accessible. She tried to smile but gave up when it felt forced. Returning to what was safe, she gestured to the ice pack. "You need to keep that on or the swelling won't go down. Tomorrow, your jaw will be sore," she advised, grabbing her purse to leave. "Good night, Mr. Halvorsen."

SAMMY WATCHED AS AUBREY LEFT, bothered by her stiff manner with him. She persisted in calling him *Mr. Halvorsen,* which made him feel like an old man, and she made sure there was an invisible line between them that she didn't even come close to crossing. *That's a good thing,* his inner voice reminded, but it still didn't sit right with him. He was a lady killer of the first rate but this woman was immune to his charms. Well, to be fair, he hadn't really turned up the wattage when it came to her. He wasn't attracted to her sort, anyway. And what sort was she? the voice challenged. *Not easy to reel in,* he answered darkly. Pressing the ice pack to his face, he allowed a groan since he was alone. He suffered the pain while Aubrey was there but now…shit, that hurt.

So Aubrey was a twin, he mused. Interesting. He couldn't imagine two of her running around. She mentioned they were nothing alike. Did that mean her sister was prone to giggling, flashing bright pearly smiles and flirting? He tried to picture Aubrey being like that and it was too much for his meager imagination, not to mention the headache that had begun to pulse behind his eyeball. He sighed and tossed the ice pack in the sink to melt. It was probably a good thing Aubrey was a little on the uptight side. If pressed, he'd have to admit she wasn't hard on the eyes. When she wasn't scowling at him, that was.

CHAPTER FIVE

AUBREY GRIPPED THE PHONE a little tighter and pressed her lips together to keep the distressed sound in her brain from escaping through her mouth.

"Mother, you hate the country," she reminded Barbie, silently wondering how on earth she'd been found. Then she remembered a short conversation with Arianna before she'd left, mentioning the small California town of Emmett's Mill. "And you'd really hate it here. There is nothing but trees and country folk, two things that you find little to recommend. Besides, aren't you supposed to be opening the Manhattan apartment for the season?" she asked, almost desperately.

"Aubrey, if I didn't know better I'd say you were trying to keep me from visiting," Barbie said with a sniff. "I am your mother. It's my duty to see what you're about, even if you've decided to exile yourself to the sticks of California."

The way she said *California* made it sound as though she'd just compared it to Tijuana.

"I'm not exiling myself, Mother," Aubrey said

between gritted teeth. "I wanted a change in scenery and Emmett's Mill seemed a nice getaway from the city."

"Yes, but did you truly need to go so far? You could have easily taken in the country in the Hamptons, although this time of year it's dreadful, as you know, but still it would've been preferable to this…what is the place called, Everest Hill?"

"Emmett's Mill," Aubrey corrected and mentally counted to ten.

"Whatever. What's with the fascination with this town? I'd never even heard of it until Arianna mentioned that's where you were. All this time when you said you wanted a change of scenery I thought you meant you wanted to go to Europe for a bit."

Aubrey felt truly invaded with her mother poking and prodding at her personal reasons for moving and it chafed no end. She wasn't about to tell her mother that she fell in love with Emmett's Mill through the pages of a magazine. *American Photographic* had featured Emmett's Mill in one of their annual Twenty Best Places To Live and Aubrey had worn the pages thin from the many times she'd gazed at the images, wishing she could just insert herself into those colorful, quaint photos. Everything in that pictorial had seemed so much better than the life she was living at the time. Of course, that was around the time that her relationship with Derek had started to unravel. Anything might've seemed like Eden as long as it was far from New York.

"It doesn't matter what brought me here, Mother," she said a bit sharply. "This is my home now and I love it."

"No need to get snippy, Aubrey," her mother admonished. "I was only curious. It just seems so random, that's all."

"Well, perhaps it was but now I'm quite happy."

"Excellent. Then you'll enjoy showing us the sights."

Aubrey knew that the moment her mother stepped foot in Emmett's Mill she was likely to declare there were no sights to see, so Aubrey figured it was best to avoid the whole fiasco of a visit in the first place. She tried a different route to dissuade her mother from her plan to visit, and by *visit* she meant berate Aubrey constantly for ruining her life and by proxy Barbie's life. "Besides, Mother, I really don't have time to visit. I have a full-time job as a nanny for this adorable little boy and so it would be a wasted trip. And I thought you and Arianna had plans to redecorate the apartment? You know that will take at least a few months just to agree on the designer."

Arianna and Barbie always quibbled over taste and style, sending more than one designer running away in frustration at their inability to come to an agreement on anything from textiles to color. The very idea of being caught in their web of misery was enough to make Aubrey want to live in a cave.

"Oh, Aubrey," Barbie said in distaste. "Being a glorified babysitter is not what anyone would call a career. You're an Ivy League graduate for crying out loud. If you're not going to use your good looks to their full potential and snag a suitable husband—which really, you should give another thought to as you're not getting any younger—then you might as well find a way to put that ridiculous degree of yours to use."

"I am putting that degree to good use, Mother," she said, her blood pressure rising with each syllable dripping with disdain from her mother's professionally plumped lips. "I have a degree in child psychology and a minor in child development. I guess you could say I'm an expert in the field of raising children to be happy, well-adjusted adults."

"Darling, a piece of paper on the wall does not make you an expert in raising children when you've never had one of your own," Barbie remarked offhandedly. "And since you can't have children—someday you'll realize what a blessing that is—then it's a bit like someone trying to say they can pilot a plane because they've mastered a video simulation. Surely you can see the logic in that."

Why didn't she just hang up? Aubrey actually pictured slamming the phone down so hard that her mother's ears rang like church bells on a Sunday morning. But she didn't. Instead she simply remained silent, locked inside her own head while her mother ranted and raved about how her daughter was withering on the vine, going on as if they were in the 1800s and Aubrey was going to die a spinster. Oh, for shame!

"I have to go, Mother," she broke in, unable to take

another minute, but she had to be sure that she'd dissuaded her mother from boarding a plane to come to Emmett's Mill. "I promise to visit during the holidays," she offered, hoping that little white lie was enough to satisfy Barbie for now. She'd think of another excuse not to go home later.

"Truly?" Barbie asked, clearly suspicious. "You're not just saying that to get me off the phone?"

Damn, the woman was onto her. She faked a light laugh. "Mother...please. Would I do that?"

"Arianna would and you're exactly alike," Barbie said, sounding a little hurt, but Aubrey was too impatient to get away from the sound of her mother's voice in her ear to care.

"We are not alike and you know it," Aubrey said.

"All right, maybe you're a little more...considerate, but only by a smidge," Barbie conceded grudgingly. Then her tone brightened. "Oh, if you can make it for Christmas you can go to the Buchanan party with us. You know how Brett always had a thing for you. He became a doctor, you know."

Brett Buchanan had grown up to be a dog. Any woman who had the misfortune to bring him home was bound to catch fleas...or something else. She shuddered openly. "No thanks. Not interested in dating anyone, Mother. Not right now. I'm trying to focus on getting myself together first."

"Fine. Suit yourself. I'll be in touch."

And the line went blissfully dead. No endearments,

no warm goodbyes, just a click and then nothing. She tried to imagine what it'd be like to have a mother who was actually warm and loving, prone to giving big full-body hugs instead of air kisses and awkward pats on the hand as a way of communicating affection. But then, what was the point of conjuring fantasy when it had no chance of becoming reality?

Thoughts going rapidly downhill along with her mood, she made quick work of getting dressed and headed to the Halvorsen home for work. The memory of Ian's sweet face brightened her disposition and pushed the sour reminder of her mother's conversation far from her mind.

AUBREY WAS IN THE LIVING ROOM thumbing through a magazine while Ian played on a quilted blanket on the floor when there was a knock at the door.

Giving Ian a smile, she opened the door to find Annabelle on the other side. Sammy's sister-in-law lifted a bag and smiled warmly. "I have Ian's milk delivery," she said as Aubrey ushered her in.

"Oh, good. He drank the last batch this morning."

Annabelle started putting the plastic bags filled with milk into the freezer so they'd stay fresh longer and then when that was finished, she seemed inclined to chat so Aubrey invited her to stay. In truth, Aubrey was curious to know more about Dana, and Annabelle seemed a logical place to start since Sammy wasn't up to sharing.

"So how's it going with Ian?" Annabelle asked,

pausing to pluck the boy from the floor to hold him close. She placed a smacking kiss against his forehead and he gurgled with delight, trying to grab on to the burnished-copper curls falling around her shoulders. "Is he giving you any trouble?"

"Not at all, he's a wonderful baby," Aubrey said, smiling at her easy and affectionate way with Ian. It was apparent Annabelle loved Ian deeply and it touched Aubrey to see that open fondness. "I wondered if you might be able to tell me what Dana was like," she said, watching Annabelle closely for any signs that she might've stepped into forbidden territory. When Annabelle merely smiled, her eyes warm with the memory of her friend, Aubrey knew she'd come to the right source.

"Dana was strong," Annabelle started, her voice nostalgic. "She overcame a lot from her childhood to build a better life. She was smart and funny, but she was allergic to bullshit. She didn't dish it out and certainly didn't let anyone give it to her. She'd be the first person to call you on it if you tried. She's the reason me and Dean got together."

"Really? How so?" Aubrey asked, tucking her feet under her in anticipation of a good story. Lord, she was a sucker for a sweet romance. "If you wouldn't mind sharing…I'd love to hear what happened."

Annabelle grinned and blushed a little but seemed open to sharing. "Well, Dana had already married Sammy when I came to Emmett's Mill. She knew from the start that Dean was my perfect match even if we were both bound and determined to muck it up. I fought it pretty hard but in the end…he turned out to be my knight in shining armor and I couldn't resist." Annabelle got a dreamy look in her eyes but then must've realized how silly she looked and blushed deeper. "I must sound like a total sap. But it's true. Those Halvorsen men… good stock. Every single one of them."

"I heard that Josh punched Samuel…do you know why?" she asked, hesitant to bring it up, but her curiosity was burning a hole in her brain.

"Um, yeah, I did hear about that," Annabelle said but seemed reluctant to elaborate. She caught Aubrey's searching gaze and then said, "Well, you have to understand that Sammy hasn't been himself since Dana died. He's been…uh…regressing."

"Regressing?" She frowned. "How do you mean?"

Annabelle looked conflicted. "Before he met Dana he was a bit of a skirt chaser if you know what I mean. But he changed his ways once he fell in love with Dana. She wouldn't put up with his crap and when he realized she was going to walk away from him, he straightened up right quick and begged her to marry him. She told him to pound sand and made a point to go out every night and have fun. It killed him. But getting a dose of his own medicine was just the thing he needed to get his head together."

"Sounds like Dana knew how to get what she wanted," Aubrey murmured, silently in awe of Sammy's deceased wife.

Annabelle sighed. "Yeah…but sometimes she went after what she wanted without considering the consequences."

"Do you mean Ian?" Aubrey asked, almost holding her breath. All she knew of Dana's death was that it was an unfortunate incident that occurred during childbirth.

Annabelle nodded. "Dana wanted a baby so badly she ignored what the doctors had told her. Sammy…he tried to talk sense into her but she desperately wanted a child with Sammy. And so she finally got pregnant."

"Why couldn't she have babies?"

"Dana was diabetic. It's not something she ever talked about, in fact, for a long time she hid it from Sammy until he caught her giving herself an insulin dose early in their relationship. She didn't like anyone to know about her private stuff and the diabetes was something she preferred to fight on her own with little interference. The pregnancy took everything out of her. She died from kidney failure."

"Oh." Aubrey's eyes watered for a woman she'd never known but had a feeling she was beginning to understand. If she were given a chance to have a child…she'd do what she could to make that happen. She knew the pain of being denied something so badly desired. "Did she get to see him before she died?"

Annabelle squeezed her eyes shut for a brief moment and Aubrey knew she was holding back tears. She felt bad for reminding her of such a painful memory but she hungered for glimpses into this woman's life and she couldn't bring herself to stop her. Annabelle drew a deep breath before answering. "Briefly. She opened her eyes long enough to make sure he was all right. She heard his cries and then she was gone."

"I'm so sorry," she said, not quite sure what to say. It was such a tragic story but it only made her want to know more about the woman who had managed to tame the wild ways of the youngest Halvorsen brother. "She sounds like a wonderful friend and I have no doubt she would've been a good mother."

"Thank you," Annabelle accepted the polite sentiment at face value and then, wiping at her eyes, she gave Ian another quick kiss and gently returned him to his toys. "It was nice chatting with you but I should get back to my own little one. Perhaps you could bring Ian over for a playdate sometime? Or maybe when Sammy is ready to pull his head out of his ass you could join us for a barbecue before the weather gets too cold."

"Oh, that's sweet but I wouldn't want to intrude on a family barbecue. I'm just the nanny."

Annabelle smiled, her gaze wistful. "Don't sell yourself short. You have the most important job ever—helping to raise my best friend's baby. Ian needs someone like you because right now...Sammy is being an idiot."

Aubrey smiled at the blunt honesty in Annabelle's statement. She liked this woman, even if she was a tad intimidated by her lush curves and natural sparkling beauty that made everything her mother and sister did to retain that youthful glow look cheap and plastic. To

Annabelle's invitation, she offered a compromise. "We'll see how it goes. Right now, it's not likely Samuel would appreciate me horning in on his family. He seems pretty territorial about certain things." If he went crazy over an apple tree she could only imagine how nuts he'd go if she showed up at a family get-together. "Besides, to be honest, I don't like to blur the lines between employer and employee."

A new level of respect and understanding brightened Annabelle's gaze as she said, "That's something I can appreciate. Someday I'll have to tell you the whole story of how I met my husband. Suffice to say…I was once his office manager."

At that Annabelle smiled like an imp and walked out the door.

Aubrey pursed her lips and considered Annabelle's parting statement. So Annabelle had once been Dean's employee. Well, that was not a situation she was likely to emulate. She'd already touched that particular hot stove and she had the burn marks to prove it.

SAMMY DIDN'T WANT TO but there was no way he could avoid answering his mother's summons. She'd called him on his cell asking him to stop by on some fake need for his assistance—which was complete and utter bull and they both knew it—but he was raised to be a gentleman by a woman with a firm hand. So, as soon as work was finished he headed over to his parents' place to see what was up.

"Sammy, my sweet boy," Mary said, smiling as he walked through the door. "Thank you for stopping by. Come, tell me how your new nanny is working out."

He glanced around, hands on his hips, but tried to keep his annoyance at bay. "Ma, you said you needed me to move something…a dresser or an armoire…"

She waved away his words and gestured for him to sit down. "Oh, your father already took care of it. I told him not to but he wouldn't listen. Anyway, it's done but since you're here, let's chat."

Arrgggh. He didn't want to chat but he took a seat and stretched his long legs out in front of him, resigned to his mother's interrogation. "What do you want to chat about?" he asked with a sigh.

"Are you and Aubrey getting along?"

Sammy shrugged. "Good enough. She's punctual and seems to like the kid."

Mary's expression darkened, and he knew a lecture was on the horizon, one he had no interest in listening to.

"Samuel, this has to stop. The boy has a name," she reminded him and he sighed in annoyance. She leaned forward in her chair and pinned him with a glower. "Don't give me that look. Your brothers have told me all about the nonsense that's been going on and it has to stop. Your boy needs you."

"Ma, I'm doing the best that I can," he said bitterly. "What more do you want? I provide for him, make sure he's fed and clothed. That nanny you made me hire is costing a fortune when I probably could've found a day care in town that would've worked just as well. Besides, he's just a baby. He couldn't care less if I'm around, as long as his belly is full and his bed is warm."

"You're acting like an idiot," Mary said, disappointment etched on her face. "I can't believe how selfish you've become. What happened to my sweet, loving boy?" she asked, her tone sad.

At that Sammy got to his feet, no longer able to take another minute of this torture. He and his ma had always been close but he needed distance right now. "I gotta go. Take care of yourself, Ma. Give Pops my love."

He stalked from the house, the heavy weight pulling on his heart a familiar feeling by now. He almost didn't know what he'd do without it as his constant companion.

CHAPTER SIX

IT WAS SATURDAY, HER DAY OFF, and Aubrey was curled in a chair she'd bought at a yard sale with a book in her hand. She loved nothing more than losing herself in the lives of other people, where she knew that happy endings were possible. This particular book featured a sheikh with a terrible attitude toward women—something she'd never tolerate in real life but absolutely adored reading about—and a feisty heroine who was perfect in nearly every way except for her deplorable taste in men. She sighed with delight as she approached the love scene.

Then just as the sheikh was peeling the clothes from his naughty secretary, Aubrey's front door flew open, scaring the daylights out of her and reminding her quite quickly that just because she lived in the country didn't mean she should leave her doors unlocked.

"Oh, God, it's worse than we thought."

The sound of her sister's voice sent spikes of dismay through her when she realized who was walking through her door and critiquing her home.

"Arianna?" Aubrey said, jumping from her chair, her book forgotten. "Mother? What are you doing here?"

Arianna pursed her lips in distaste at the decor in the small rented house but leaned toward Aubrey for an air kiss, which Aubrey reluctantly reciprocated. "Aubrey, darling...*what* are you doing? This is worse than the time you sequestered yourself in that dingy little art house college in San Francisco where no one bathed or waxed their armpits." Arianna shuddered delicately and Aubrey nearly giggled at the memory of that escapade. That one was true. For a time Aubrey fancied herself a painter and figured she ought to immerse herself in the culture of the artistically inclined of the Bay Area set, which had translated into infrequent bathing, little to no waxing or shaving and lots of late-night discussions about existentialism and the dogma of organized religion. It was fun...for a time. As much as Aubrey loved her art, in the end she wasn't prepared to give up that much of her personal hygiene. "I grew a lot at that place," she said with a shrug, enjoying her sister's look of disgust. "Besides, sometimes you have to step outside your comfort zone to learn more about yourself."

"I know enough about myself. I don't need smelly roommates to figure it out," Arianna said as their mother crossed into the living room, her expression appalled.

"This is ridiculous. Are you trying to kill me?" Barbie said, exasperated. "If any of our friends could see the way you're living...we'd be a laughingstock. Do you ever think of anyone but yourself, Aubrey? Honestly!"

"I thought I told you not to come," Aubrey said, feeling sullen and put upon by her mother and sister's criticism.

"There's nothing here you will enjoy, not even for a short visit. I told you I'd come home for the holidays."

"You and I both knew you were lying," Barbie said, glancing around at the bare white walls and the brown shag carpet that was hardly new but at least it was clean. "I'm worried about you. It's a mother's duty to see to her daughter's welfare."

Since when? Aubrey didn't buy her mother's explanation. There had to be some other reason Barbie and Arianna had both decided to brave the wild, untamed regions of the California foothills. Then Aubrey was sharply annoyed at herself for wondering what that reason was when she knew full well to dig for the answer would only encourage them to stay longer.

"Mom, I'm not a child any longer. I don't need you hovering over me, trying to make sure I don't screw up." Aubrey's temper began to rise until Arianna laughed and surprisingly took her side against their mother.

"Mom, she's right. We're guests in her home. We need to be respectful of her space. Forgive us, Aubrey, darling. We're just…taken aback at the different way you've chosen to live your life. That's all."

Aubrey stared in suspicion at her sister, not trusting this turnabout at all. She wanted to trust her sister, but there was a lot of water under that bridge and frankly, Aubrey wasn't into jumping in feetfirst without a life jacket. The waters that ran beneath that bridge had strong and dangerous currents.

"So to what do I owe this auspicious visit?" Aubrey

asked with a sigh as she returned to her chair, placing a bookmark inside her book for later. "What happened to the idea that you were going to redecorate the apartment?"

Arianna and Barbie exchanged looks and Aubrey felt a frisson of alarm at the suddenly nervous twitch of her sister's fingers as she played with the strap of her Prada bag. "What's going on?" she asked, looking from one to the other with growing trepidation.

Barbie silenced Arianna with a warning look and gave Aubrey a bright smile that only made Aubrey even more apprehensive. Her mother was not the sunny type. The only time she'd ever seen her mother smile with pure joy was when her father agreed to buy her the Jaguar she'd been pining for. "You have such a suspicious nature, darling. Nothing is afoot. We tired of the city and wanted to get some fresh air."

Aubrey narrowed her gaze at her mother, smelling a pile of B.S. in spite of the expensive perfume her mother wore. "The air is just as fresh, perhaps even more so in the Hamptons, where you prefer to vacation, I might add, so I'll ask again… What's going on?"

Arianna looked intensely uncomfortable and Aubrey had a sinking feeling it had nothing to do with the rustic decor. Finally, Arianna couldn't hold back any longer and burst into tears, startling them both as she covered her face and wept.

Aubrey went to her twin and wrapped her arms around her, bewildered. Arianna never cried. "Mother?" A horrible thought came to her and concern overrode her irritation at the sudden visit. "Are either one of you sick?" Thoughts of cancer or leukemia or a brain tumor of some sort raced through her mind but Barbie's flustered and annoyed expression at Arianna's outburst lessened that fear. Surely their mother wouldn't look so aggravated if there was something as dreadful as cancer in the family.

Barbie sighed and looked as if she had a bad taste in her mouth. "No one is sick but we do have a bit of a *situation*. It's just a temporary one, I'm sure," she said stiffly. "But it seems your father has deemed it necessary to restrict our funds."

Funds? For a moment Aubrey couldn't comprehend what her mother was saying until Arianna made a loud sniffling noise.

"He's cut us off!" Arianna exclaimed, before burying her face in Aubrey's shoulder.

Barbie's pinched expression made Aubrey's blood run cold. Was it possible? "What do you mean?" she asked.

"Well, he—"

"Daddy is divorcing Mom and he's cut off both of our allowances. My Visa no longer works and my checking account is practically empty. He's leaving us with nothing," Arianna wailed.

Barbie looked stricken and Aubrey realized this was not a joke. In fact, Barbie looked ready to pass out. Aubrey disentangled herself from her sister's clutches and led her mother to the sofa, where she sat gingerly. For the first time ever, Barbie looked fragile.

"Mother? Is this true?" she asked quietly.

"I don't know what's gotten into your father. He's refusing to talk to me and I don't know if he means to divorce me but it's true that he's cut us off. I couldn't take the shame of it so we decided to leave until your father could come to his senses." She looked to Aubrey, her eyes filling with moisture. "I know you don't want us here but…we had nowhere else to go."

Aubrey was at a loss for words. She had to talk with her dad to get to the root of the problem. Her father was not a cruel man, in fact, he was quite loving. She knew there was money in her own bank account as she'd just checked her balance yesterday and there was the healthy amount, which her father's accountant always deposited at the beginning of the month for her allowance. Unlike her sister, who burned through her money and always asked for more, Aubrey almost always had some left over, which she moved into a savings account.

"Of course you can stay," Aubrey said, troubled by this turn of events. "We'll get to the bottom of this and everything will be fine. Did Daddy say that he was divorcing you, Mother?" she asked.

Barbie gave a delicate sniff before answering. "Not exactly but he's been very distant and cold. Not like his usual self. When I told him my plans to renovate, he actually *yelled* at me."

That *was* odd. Her dad rarely raised his voice, not

even when it came to his wife's voracious spending habits. But truly, Aubrey never thought her mother's shopping was a problem but perhaps it was. The stock market had plummeted, and she wasn't sure if her father's portfolio had been affected. Harold Rose was the financial advisor to some of the biggest names in the Manhattan society circles. He worked with big money and pocketed a fair share of it for his services. It was nearly impossible to conceive that they were broke.

She patted her mother's knee reassuringly. "I'm sure it'll all be fine. We'll figure out what's going on. In the meantime, you and Arianna can share the spare bedroom. It has a queen-size bed so it should be fine."

Both Arianna and Barbie exchanged looks. Then her mother said, "Darling, we were hoping that perhaps you could call your father. You were always so close. I doubt he would refuse a call from you."

It was not a request she could turn down, not with both her mother and sister peering at her with such hope in their eyes, but it made her distinctly uncomfortable to be placed in such a position. "Of course I'll try," she said. Their expressions of relief mirrored one another. "But he might not take my call, either. It's obvious Daddy is going through something… maybe he just wants a little space to think things through."

"Perhaps," Barbie said, though it was clear she wasn't entirely convinced. Barbie gestured with a slight movement of her hand. "If you wouldn't mind, dear…"

"Right." She grabbed her cell phone and dialed her dad's number. It went to voice mail. She frowned but felt slightly relieved even as she shook her head to her sister and mother. "Voice mail," she said. She would've just left it at that until she could try again later but the crashing of their hopes was too much to take and her grudging concern for the situation dictated another try.

"Who are you calling now?" her mother inquired. "I've already tried all our friends. It's like he's simply disappeared!"

"Phil," she answered, chewing her bottom lip.

Barbie's expression soured. "That little bean counter won't tell you anything," she said, wrinkling her nose as if she'd just smelled something vile. "He's always hated me. Constantly filling your father's head with lies and planting little seeds of doubt. It's a wonder he hasn't managed to derail our marriage before now."

"You don't know that Phil has done anything or said anything to influence whatever Daddy is doing. Just calm down a minute and let me see what I can find out."

He picked up and Aubrey decided to take the call in private.

Once in her bedroom she wasted little time and asked Phil what was going on.

"Phil, my mother and sister are here claiming my dad has cut them off. What's happening? Is everything all right?"

Phil Burrough, a nice enough man for an accountant, in spite of the low opinion her mother was fond of sharing, sighed on the other end before answering, as if he were shouldering an enormous weight. "It's not good, Aubrey," he admitted and a cold shaft of fear pierced her heart. "Your mother and sister have run your father into the ground with their incessant shopping. I've been telling your father for years to get them under control but now we've come to this and it's too late."

Aubrey's hand trembled. "What do you mean?"

"He's selling all but one house, including the New York apartment, the town house in Martha's Vineyard and, of course, the cottage in the Hamptons. It's all going to be sold to produce cash for the crippling credit card debt your mother and sister have created."

"But Daddy has always had plenty of money," Aubrey protested, feeling sick to her stomach. "I don't understand. How could this have happened?"

"Times have changed, recent investments have not panned out the way we'd hoped. There are many people in this position who made similar investments that went up in smoke with this wretched economy. Some people have lost whole fortunes. At least your father has some assets he can liquidate."

Liquidate. The very word did something terrible to the contents of her lower intestine. She could only imagine what her mother and sister were feeling. "Where's Daddy now? I can't get hold of him," she said.

"He asked me not to disclose his location right now.

He needs to think and he can't do that with your sister and mother harping at him. I know you wouldn't tell them but he doesn't want to put you in the middle."

"Plausible deniability," Aubrey said with a twist of her lips even though she felt numb inside. "It's a little late for that, Phil. Why didn't Daddy tell anyone that we were struggling? Maybe if he'd told my mother..."

"He tried."

"Be that as it may, it's completely unacceptable that he would just disappear like this. *Unacceptable,* Phil. If you know where he is, please tell me. I have to speak to him right away. This is downright cruel."

"I'm sorry, Aubrey. I can't do that. He's my client and he's asked me to keep his confidence. Just know that he is safe and he'll be in touch soon. In the meantime, perhaps you could teach your sister and mother how to be a little more frugal. That's a skill that will come in handy in the coming days."

They were poor. She'd never truly relied on her allowance but it was nice to know that if she'd ever found herself in a bind, it would be there. Suddenly the distaste her mother had always felt for the seemingly mild-mannered accountant didn't seem so unwarranted. Perhaps she was imagining it, but she detected a faint amount of smugness in his last statement. She ignored his advice and instead said coolly, "Please tell my father to call me as soon as possible."

"I will do that," Phil said, then added, "I know you're better with your money but don't let your sister or mother know how much you have banked or they'll drain you dry just like they did your father."

"You worry about getting my father to come to his senses. I can handle my mother and sister."

"Yes, well, I recall your father making a similar statement and look how that has turned out."

Aubrey clicked off without further comment. She took a moment to regroup before facing her mother and sister, who were sitting in the living room, no doubt turning their nose up at their new temporary living accommodations even as they waited for word.

"Did you talk to Daddy?" Arianna asked, her eyes red. "Is he going to send us some money?"

Aubrey took a deep breath and prayed for strength. "Daddy is MIA right now but it sounds like he's got a pretty good reason."

Barbie stiffened and narrowed her stare. "What does that mean?"

"Mother…Phil says you and Arianna have been living beyond your means for years and it's finally caught up to you. Daddy hasn't so much cut you off as…you're broke."

Arianna looked ready to puke. "What?"

Barbie looked away with a negative shake of her head. "Impossible. He's just saying that because he's never liked me. Your father should've fired him years ago."

"I don't see what Phil would have to gain by lying. They're selling the properties to pay off your credit card debt."

Barbie jumped to her feet. "What? He's doing what? This is an outrage! He can't do that without my permission! I furnished and decorated them. I put my blood and sweat into turning those shells into homes for our family. He can't just sell them right out from underneath me. Half of those houses are mine!"

"As is half of the debt," Aubrey said sharply. Barbie's mouth pinched but she returned to the sofa, only this time she did not sit gingerly but rather plopped in a rather undignified manner. Aubrey struggled for patience, not wanting to be cruel but recognizing this was perhaps a blessing in disguise. Money had never made anyone happy and that included the Rose family. "It's going to be okay. We're going to be fine. I mean, the way I see it, there's a silver lining to this cloud."

"Oh? And what would that be?" Arianna asked, her red-rimmed eyes staring at Aubrey with withering coolness. "I'd love to hear how losing everything that ever meant anything to us is a good thing."

"We're just normal people now. No more ridiculous parties, or redecorating for the umpteenth time or trying to hang out with people we hate anyway. Frankly, I'm relieved."

At first she said it for her mother's sake but then she realized that she meant it. No more pretending. No more suffering through shallow, narcissistic blowhards for the sake of appearances. *Hallelujah.*

Of course, judging by the leaching of color from both her sister's and mother's faces it was easy to see they didn't agree. For them, it was probably the equivalent of the Apocalypse raining down.

"We're ruined," Arianna said in a hoarse groan, turning to her mother and gripping her by the arm. "You have to fix this! What am I supposed to do?"

It wasn't funny but Aubrey had to cover her smile if only to keep from yelling at them both for the situation that they'd put them all in. "Arianna, you have a degree. Put it to use and you'll be fine," she said, offering what she thought was perfectly sensible advice, but Arianna reacted with a horrified hiss.

"Are you saying I should get a job?" she asked.

"Well, that's what normal people do who haven't been raised like overprivileged princesses," Aubrey retorted drily. "Why'd you go to college if you never had plans to start a career?"

Arianna's mouth formed a perfectly pinched moue as she answered archly, "The same reason most of those with our kind of pedigree do—to find a husband."

"If that's the case, it would seem you missed the mark. You are still perfectly single," Aubrey said with good humor that was completely lost on either her sister or mother. They both stared with hard expressions. Aubrey sighed. "Whatever. The situation being as it is, we just have to make the best of it. Daddy will call when he's ready. In the meantime, you are welcome to stay as my guests. Feel free to take a walk around the property, take a nap or freshen up. I assume your flight was exhausting."

On the outside, she may have looked calm and collected, but inside Aubrey was shaking. She couldn't give in to tears or else her mother and sister would fall to pieces in worse fashion than they were already doing. So, in a show of restraint, Aubrey returned to her chair where her book remained, waiting, and she opened the pages to lose herself in the exotic fantasy where alpha men rescued their women, their snobby relatives rarely made house calls and their fathers did not abandon them.

"MA'S FIT TO BE TIED WITH YOU lately," Dean said, throwing a log into his truck while Sammy hefted the ax to slice into the next round of wood. "She's worrying herself to death."

Sammy spared a second to give Dean a look that said *shut up* and then brought the ax whistling down to cleave the round in two. "She'll get over it," he said, gritting his teeth against the sudden pull in his shoulder. He rotated his cuff before hefting the ax again. "She'll find some committee or cause to take up and she'll forget all about my attitude or whatever I've done to put a bee in her bonnet."

"Doubtful. You're her baby. Maybe you could go and apologize. Put her mind at rest."

"C'mon, Dean, you and I both know that ain't gonna happen," he said. "Let's just get this done."

Dean and Sammy had gone in together on an order of two cords of wood, and Dean was there to collect his share. Sammy had forgotten about the wood coming but he wasn't about to keep a pile of wood in his yard until he and Dean were on better terms. That could take all year. So he'd gritted his teeth and invited his brother over. Annabelle was in the house watching Ian so the two could get the chore done without worrying about the kid.

It was several minutes later when Dean started talking again. "Sammy, I know how it feels to lose the woman you love," Dean said, the knowledge in his voice only making Sammy intensely aware of the void inside his heart. "It might help to talk to someone."

"Why? It won't bring her back," Sammy said bitterly. "It'll just serve to remind me that she's gone. I don't want to talk about her to anyone. I don't want to acknowledge that she's gone."

"I know how you feel and you're right, nothing will bring her back—even ignoring the fact that she's gone and not coming back."

Sammy glared at his brother, hating that he was so damn right. "Cut me some slack, Dean. She's only been gone six months. My whole life has been turned upside down and I don't know which end is up anymore. All I know is I have to focus on getting up each morning and facing the day because all I want to do is crawl in a hole and disappear."

"What about Ian? Do you think about him when you're lost in your own grief?"

"Ian doesn't care about anything except a clean diaper and a full belly," Sammy said sullenly, not quite answering. He didn't have the balls to admit that when he was locked in those dark places, he refused to think about his son. It was easier that way.

"You're wrong," Dean said. "And you're missing out on the one thing that could bring you back from the edge. Something to cling to."

"Yeah, like what?"

"Your son, you blooming idiot," Dean said, losing his temper.

"Screw you," Sammy said, his resentment a thick paste on his tongue. "You don't know what it's like to try to raise a kid by yourself. By the time Beth died, Brandon was a teenager. He was self-sufficient. Ian is a baby. I don't know the first thing about raising a kid. I've been thinking…maybe he'd be better off without me."

"Now you're just talking stupid," Dean said, eliciting a scowl from Sammy. Damn self-righteous asshole, Sammy thought and it must've been written all over his face, for Dean's expression tightened with anger. "The only thing you're doing is feeling sorry for yourself. Yes, your wife died. We all loved Dana and she brought out the best in you, but you don't have the luxury of climbing into that grave with her so put on big-girl panties and stop your sniveling. Everyone's had enough. And you treating Ma like you did…that's not okay. She cares about you, even though you're acting like a spoiled little prick, and she's just trying to help."

"Yeah, well everyone ought to just stop trying to help," Sammy shot back with a sneer. "You ever think maybe I don't want anyone's help? I just want to be left alone but that's damn near impossible in this family because everyone has to have their noses shoved so far up everyone else's asses that they could probably tell what the other person had for lunch!"

Dean pulled off his gloves and went toe-to-toe with Sammy. "Yeah, well, maybe if you'd man up we wouldn't have to follow you around wondering if you're going to remember that you have to feed and clothe your infant son. You want to know why Ma dragged that poor woman from her quilting circle into your home? Because she was terrified that you might do something stupid to Ian."

"What?"

"Yeah, you heard me. And can you blame her? You won't hold him, you treat him like he's garbage that's been dragged into your house, and you never try to comfort him when he cries. For crying out loud, Sam...do you know Annabelle's been expressing breast milk for your son so that he can get the best possible start in life? My wife is exhausting herself trying to produce enough milk for our daughter and your son. What are you doing for Ian aside from assuring that he grows up with a father who acts like he hates him just for being born? I'll tell you what you're doing—a big fat nothing. You can't be bothered with the care of your son because you've got better things to do...such as screwing every skirt in town with no regard as to how it looks to other people. Ever heard of discretion? How about at least putting on a front that you're grieving?"

Sammy roared and tossed the ax, hurtling into his brother, taking him down hard.

Dean grunted as he landed on the ground and Sammy swung wildly, catching Dean in the jaw with a sharp crack with his knuckles.

"Just leave me the hell alone!" he managed to yell right before Dean landed a good one right in the nose. He felt his nose pop and blood gushed from his nostrils. Groaning, he rolled away from Dean to stagger to his feet. "You broke my nose," Sammy said accusingly as Dean climbed to his feet, rubbing his jaw. "I hope I dislocated your jaw, you son of a bitch," he added with a glower.

Dean worked his jaw and squinted against the sunlight. "Sorry to disappoint you. Still seems to work okay. You all right?" he asked.

Sammy waved away his concern, embarrassed as hell that he'd just gotten whupped by another of his brothers. At the rate he was going, he was liable to get licked by his Pops next. "I'm fine," he said tersely. "You said your piece, now let's get this shit done so we can get the hell away from each other."

Dean shook his head in disappointment and thankfully agreed that they had nothing more to say to one another for the moment. The rest of the time was spent in silence as they split, hauled and stacked wood for the coming winter.

When Dean and Annabelle left, it was late afternoon and Sammy had more than aching hands to deal with. His nose throbbed but that was the least of his worries.

Dean had hit a nerve. And his heart had taken the biggest beating of all.

He was a shitty father. Sinking into his battered recliner, he stared at Ian as he played on the floor, gurgling his contentment and batting at the play structure placed in front of him, and Sammy fought a wave of shame.

"You deserve better, kid," he acknowledged softly. The question was, did he have it in him to be the father Ian deserved?

Wiping gingerly at his nose, he wished he had the answer.

CHAPTER SEVEN

AUBREY WAS NERVOUS ABOUT leaving her sister and mother behind while she attended her Quilters Brigade meeting so she invited them to come along. The reaction was entertaining—if you weren't easily offended.

"We're stuck in hillbilly hell and you want to rub salt in the wound by dragging us to some local event where everyone will stare at us for being strangers?" Barbie asked with a horrified sniff. "I don't think so. I'd rather wear white pants before Memorial Day in full view of all our friends before doing that."

"What friends?" Aubrey quipped, only mildly annoyed. "If you had real friends I would think that you'd be staying with them rather than in this—what did you call it?—hillbilly hell. But as it happens, here you are, pouting and whining but here just the same."

"You don't understand. You never did, which is why you're perfectly at home in these surroundings," Barbie said mournfully. "If I hadn't spent twenty hours in labor and seen the doctor pull you from my body I would swear you were not of my womb."

"That makes two of us," Aubrey muttered, then tried

one last time to persuade the two to come. "Listen, I know it's not your usual thing but you ought to give it a try. You know the old saying, When in Rome do as the Romans do. You might find that you enjoy it."

"Doubtful," Barbie said with a stiff expression. "But seeing as I can't sit here all day while you gallivant around the countryside I might as well make the best of it."

With a theatrical martyr-on-the-cross sigh, Barbie followed Aubrey to her car. Arianna reluctantly climbed in the backseat.

Although Aubrey only lived fifteen minutes from town, with her mother and sister in the car, complaining every mile, it seemed to take forever before Aubrey was pulling into the parking lot of the converted barn that was the meeting place for the Quilters Brigade.

Before they went in, she said, "Please keep your snobbery to a minimum. These people are quite kind and I'm still new in the community. I'd like to keep their opinion of me favorable."

"Honestly, Aubrey, you act like we're monkeys and can't be expected to know which fork to use in a formal setting," Arianna said in an irritated huff. "If I can tolerate Penelope Pritchard's insufferable presence at parties I can certainly handle a few of your hillbilly friends."

Right. Somehow Aubrey wasn't sure about that but she was hoping for the best.

When they entered, Aubrey smiled at Mary Halvorsen, Annabelle and a woman she hadn't met yet but seemed close to the Halvorsen clan. She only had a short time to wonder before for the woman came up to her, smiling warmly. "You have to be Aubrey," she said, surprising Aubrey. The woman gestured toward Mary. "I'm Tasha, Josh's wife, and I've only heard good things about you through Annabelle. She said you're a blessing to poor Ian."

"He's a wonderful baby," Aubrey said, smiling in the face of such effusive praise and open admiration. These Halvorsen women weren't hard to like, which led her to wonder about their husbands. She'd seen Josh's handiwork on Sammy's jaw but standing there next to his wife, who was beaming at her, she had a hard time figuring out the family. Apparently, punching a brother was no big deal around these circles. "Are things okay between Josh and Samuel?" she asked, her curiosity getting the better of her.

Tasha laughed off Aubrey's concern. "These days a good punch in the mouth is exactly what Sammy needs. I wouldn't worry about it. I've known Sammy since he was a kid and sometimes he truly deserves what he gets. Besides, that's just how they blow off steam. That's sweet that you were worried, though."

"Oh, I wasn't worried, just curious," Aubrey said, backtracking. Worried about Sammy? Not even. That man didn't need her worrying over him. Frankly, he couldn't care less what she thought of him. At least that's the impression he gave off in waves. She laughed shakily when she realized she was beginning to obsess about the man. "Well, I'm glad it hasn't come between them."

Barbie made a small noise indicating Aubrey was being rude for not introducing them and so Aubrey made quick work of it just in time for Mary to announce to the group what their next project was going to be.

"As you all know the economy has really hurt many of our community members who relied upon the construction business for their livelihood. Many people have been laid off and Christmas this year is going to be brutal. So I propose instead of making quilts—and I know this is a scandalous idea for the Brigade to consider—I thought we could knit children's blankets for the local families."

A murmur went through the crowd, prompting Mary to continue. "Yes, I know we always make a Christmas quilt and raffle it off at the annual Elks Lodge Christmas dinner, but I think we need to consider the bigger picture. There are those who don't have the money to buy a nice thick blanket to stay warm and we need to do what we can to help those who are less fortunate."

"But we always make a quilt," protested one Brigade member. "It's what we do. People expect it of us and I know there will be a lot of disappointment out there if we don't."

"Well, Betty, sometimes we have to be open to change," Mary said patiently, but there were more unhappy faces in the crowd. Mary looked annoyed that not everyone was pleased with her idea. Sammy's mother, Aubrey quickly learned, was like a bull in a china shop when she got something into her head.

"How about doing both?" Aubrey suggested and everyone swiveled to look at her, even her mother and Arianna, except their expressions were mildly amused. Now that she had the floor and Mary was regarding her with narrowed eyes, she nearly lost her nerve. "I think Mary's idea is charitable and timely but Betty is right, if people look forward to bidding on that Christmas quilt, perhaps the Brigade should protect the tradition."

Mary considered the proposal and suddenly she seemed on board, which Aubrey found to be an immense relief. She truly did not want to go head-to-head with Mary Halvorsen. "We shall put it to a vote," Mary announced to the crowd. "Everyone who would like to be involved with the Christmas quilt raise your hand." Nearly half the room raised their hand. "All right, that settles it. We will do both projects but I don't want to hear any bellyaching when fingers are cramping from all the extra work."

There was a general sense of laughter going around the room as light chuckles followed and Aubrey smiled. She felt an overwhelming sense of contentment sitting here in this room with people she hardly knew. It's funny, she spent her childhood surrounded by people of her mother and sister's ilk and never felt that she fit in and, of course, that fact was not lost on her family. She leaned over to her sister, who looked colossally bored, and said, "You ought to try quilting or knitting, it's really addicting once you get started."

Arianna gave her a sour look. "I'd rather poke a fork

in my eye than dabble in this prefeminist movement *women's work*. It's degrading, honestly," she said in a low voice so at least only Aubrey was privy to her words. "I mean, are these people caught in a time warp or something? Knitting? *Seriously?* This is all Daddy's fault."

Aubrey tried hard not to grit her teeth. If anyone was to blame for their current financial situation the culprit was sitting right beside her in designer clothes and clutching a ridiculously expensive handbag. "Arianna...don't be so bitter. It's unbecoming," Aubrey said. "Besides, doing something for others is incredibly gratifying."

"Oh, don't be so smug," Arianna said. "You're not the only one who gives to the needy. I always donate my used clothes to the celebrity auctions. They raise money for poor kids, too!"

"Throwing last season's clothing in a pile with instructions for the maid to come and take it away is not in keeping with the spirit of true charitable giving. Besides, trust me, you'll get more out of it if the hard work comes directly from your hands."

Arianna huffed, not amused or convinced. "Whatever."

Aubrey tried not to enjoy her sister's distress but for the first time ever the shoe was on the other foot and she wasn't above savoring it just a little.

The meeting concluded about an hour later and as they were leaving Mary made her way over to them.

"I didn't see either of you raise your hand for a

project," she said, smiling at both Barbie and Arianna, who suddenly wore matching horrified expressions that were hard to mask even with their incredible powers of two-faced deception. "Don't be shy now, we take all levels of experience. Before Annabelle started with the Brigade, she couldn't put together two stitches with any kind of talent, but now, she's cooking right along. How about it? Quilt or blanket?"

"Neither," they both said in unison. Aubrey jumped in to salvage the moment.

"Unfortunately, they're only staying a short time before they have to return to the east coast," she explained with a regretful expression. "So, that's why they didn't volunteer."

"Oh, I see." Mary nodded. "So what do you think of Emmett's Mill? Our family is a direct descendent of the town's founder. In fact, just a few years ago the Quilters Brigade formed a committee with the Historical Society to relocate the mill to its current place of glory where everyone can enjoy a piece of local history. You ought to take a look while you're here. It's a sight to see, for sure."

"Perhaps," Barbie said in a noncommittal way as she took in Mary's stout figure and frizzed hair that was more gray than anything else and no doubt mentally tried to calculate her age. Aubrey withheld a sigh. For all of Barbie's well-preserved middle-age, she had the warmth of an iceberg. She'd often wished for a mother just like Mary—someone who was fun, loud and protective. Instead, she got…Barbie.

But then, conversely, Barbie had been saddled with a daughter who shunned everything she believed in so perhaps they were even, Aubrey thought with a private shrug as she said her goodbyes.

"I can't stay here," Arianna announced as soon as they were back in the car. "I'll lose my mind."

Barbie shared her daughter's expression except for one notable difference. Her mother's face held a bleak mournfulness that almost made Aubrey do a double take. Her mother with real emotion? Impossible.

Barbie turned to Arianna. "We have nowhere to go. If we return home we'll be forced to make up excuses as to why we're not attending this party or that party and eventually, everyone will catch on that we're hiding something. Besides, it's likely your father has already had that detestable man of his, Phil, list our homes. People have already seen them on the market. Darling, we can't go back in this state. It'll be the ruin of us."

At that Arianna wept great, silent tears that tugged at Aubrey's heart. *Damn that twin connection.* Aubrey wanted to comfort her but what could she say? While it seemed no great loss to Aubrey, it was the end of Arianna's world and for that she needed to respect her sister's right to grieve. They rode the rest of the way home in silence.

CHAPTER EIGHT

By THE TIME AUBREY ARRIVED Monday morning, Sammy's nerves were strung so tight he was about to jump out of his skin. This happened every time he spent more than a few hours in his son's company and he didn't know what to do about it. His brothers were right, he couldn't keep avoiding his son, but frankly, he didn't know what to do with the kid. They sat and stared at each other, like a standoff of sorts, and Sammy didn't know who was winning.

"Anything I should know before you go?" Aubrey asked, the question out of her mouth before she caught a good look at his face. He'd almost forgotten about the scuffle he and his brother Dean had gotten into over the weekend until her face screwed into a distressed frown. "Are you a glutton for punishment?" she asked, coming forward to examine his face. "Who'd you make mad this time? Your mailman?"

"Another brother," Sammy said, cracking a grin that felt rusty because it was real. He was mildly amused that she cared. "It's nothing."

"Let me guess…you deserved it?"

"Yeah, you could say that," he said sheepishly. "But I think I got the message this time."

"Well, thank goodness for small favors. What would you do if you didn't have your handsome face to bend women to your will?"

He canted a sidewise glance at his nanny for her statement and her blush told him she hadn't meant to share so much. So Aubrey—the woman who rarely looked at him with more than pity and disdain—thought he was attractive? For some reason, that possibility buoyed his spirits in an unexpected way.

"You feeling sorry for me?" he asked, his tone playful. He was rewarded with a sour look and he had to choke back a laugh. "I'm just saying, you seem awful concerned about my face. I got the impression that you might support the idea of someone giving me a good whack upside the head. Don't deny it, I saw it in your expression. You'd make a terrible poker player, by the way."

She lifted her chin. "Why should I deny it? You have the manners of a donkey and sometimes the things that come out of your mouth astound me. Come to think of it, without that paltry charm of yours, you'd be lost, so if I were you I'd guard the goods."

"*Paltry?* Boy, you're just handing out the compliments this morning, aren't you?"

In spite of the insult he couldn't stop the laughter from bubbling up. It was entertaining the way she tried to keep distance between them even though he sensed there was something beneath the surface that drove her nuts. It was nice to see her a little off balance for once. "I'll keep that in mind. Thank you for your concern," he said.

"I'm not really *concerned,*" she corrected, distress causing faint lines to form on her brow that Sammy felt oddly compelled to smooth away. She had beautiful skin that seemed to glow, like it was constantly being kissed by sunlight. Everything about her made him think of pink and soft, cuddly things. For the first time, he let his gaze slide over her form when she turned away from him to busy herself in the kitchen, no doubt to get Ian his breakfast. She was small, probably a good head and a half shorter than him, which was a distinct difference between her and Dana, who had stood nearly his height. He'd actually liked that about his wife. She'd never been afraid to go toe-to-toe with him. But as a warm tingle started in the pit of his stomach he realized there was something ultrafeminine about Aubrey that he'd totally missed before. She was all soft curves and small features; even her hands, which worked efficiently to prepare Ian's rice cereal, were dainty and thin-fingered like those of a pianist. She turned back around quickly and almost caught him. Fortunately, she was too flustered to notice he'd been enjoying what he saw. "I just…well, frankly, it's annoying," she finished, surprising him.

"Annoying?"

"Yes. Grown men don't go around getting punched in the face."

He begged to differ. "Depends on what kind of men you hang around. Sometimes a good punch can knock some sense into a guy."

"Did it work for you?" she asked, peering at him with grudging curiosity. Then, she shook her head as if she couldn't support such a thing. "The human brain is not made to be knocked around like a soccer ball. You lose brain cells each time you get clocked and I'd say you need every single one, so perhaps you could quit getting punched for the sake of your son. Someday, you'll have to help him with his homework."

He couldn't think that far ahead into the future. He could barely remember the dizzying instructions she'd left on how to wash the kid's clothes. When she'd found out he'd been throwing his son's clothes in with his grubby work clothes, she'd nearly fainted. Apparently, babies need special laundry soap because their skin is so sensitive. Who knew? Speaking of…

"I think I screwed up the laundry again," he admitted, feeling the loss of every single one of those brain cells she was talking about. "I think I used too much bleach."

"What happened?"

"Well, you know that blue jumper he was wearing on Friday?" he said, and she nodded. "He pooped all over it. I mean the kid unloaded the entire contents of his gut and it was just covered. I figured since it was poop and there's all that talk about that E. coli stuff, I ought to bleach it. And then it turned a funny color."

Her open amusement did weird things to his stomach. "What's so funny?" he asked.

"You don't use regular bleach on colors. You have to use chlorine-free bleach."

He swore. "I ruined it, didn't I." It was a statement, not really a question. He already knew the answer. She giggled and his stomach did that weird flip-flop. But just as he was starting to enjoy their banter, he realized he ought to stop. He recognized this feeling and he shouldn't be feeling it for his nanny.

"Well, anyway, I just wanted to warn you, because I think the jumper wasn't the only thing that was ruined. The whole load is a mess."

"It happens," she allowed with a shrug, the warmth in her eyes something he liked seeing. He turned away and headed for the door.

"Are you going to be okay?" she asked. He glanced back at her and she gestured to his face. "It looks pretty awful."

He liked that she cared. Too much. And that messed with his head.

"I'm touched that you're worried," he said, giving her a sardonic smile he knew would irritate her. It worked.

"Don't read more into it than it is, lover boy. It's called polite consideration. Nothing more, nothing less."

"Good to know." He gave her a short wave and walked out the door.

He must really be a man-slut if he was sniffing after his nanny, for crying out loud. There were plenty of willing women out there. He certainly didn't need to be casting eyes toward the one woman who, frankly, didn't seem to like him very much.

And why was that? Well, there was that night— Sammy winced at the memory. Bringing home a strange woman, drunk to boot, after a night of tying one on…shit, he wouldn't much like him, either, if the shoe were on the other foot.

A startling thought came to him. Did Aubrey have a boyfriend? A husband somewhere? The thought stuck in his throat for no good reason. It shouldn't matter who she had waiting in the wings in her personal life, but hell, he couldn't lie, it bothered him more than a little and that just didn't make sense at all.

So when he found himself returning to the house moments later on some pretense that he'd forgotten something, he asked her the very thing he should've kept to himself.

"Are you dating anyone?"

The question took her by surprise and she stared for a moment before she recovered with an answer. "No." Her face flushed to a rosy pink shade. "What are you doing back? You're going to be late."

He ignored the question. "Married?"

She gave a little shake of her head. "No. Why?"

Huh. "Ever been close to getting married?" he asked, feeling sweat dot his hairline. He was losing his mind.

Plain and simple. Why else would he be interrogating his nanny about things that were none of his business yet he just had to know?

"What is going on?" She looked at him curiously.

He shrugged. "Nothing. I just wondered. You're good with kids. Figured you'd probably want one of your own and then it occurred to me that maybe you already do. I mean, let's face it...I don't really know much about you."

She offered a small smile acknowledging his observation but didn't elaborate, much to his chagrin, and he wasn't ready to let it go as he should.

"Why not?" he pressed.

"Why not what?" She gave him a blank stare.

"Why haven't you ever gotten married?"

She quirked an amused but wry smile. "Now you're starting to sound like my mother. Careful, I might start to think you're trying to hook me up with one of your single buddies."

He chuckled uneasily. The very thought of setting Aubrey up with one of his friends made him feel very...possessive. That was definitely a cue to stop that train from going wherever it was heading.

"Yeah, maybe," he said, playing along. "I know a few guys...." He watched for her reaction and was privately pleased when she demurred with another shake of her head. There was something there, behind her eyes, that tugged at him and made him want to wrap her in a tight hug. That would definitely be inappropriate and well, given their mostly rigid relationship with one another, probably a little odd. But it was there and he couldn't deny it. Someone had broken her heart. And not enough time had passed to dull the pain of the breakup. Suddenly, Aubrey wasn't just his nanny, she was a flesh-and-blood *woman* with a romantic past. Shutting down the thoughts that followed, he offered a noncommittal, completely ordinary and appropriate second goodbye of the morning and then practically ran to his truck.

AUBREY BUNDLED IAN UP to go to town, then made a quick pit stop to pick up her sister. She'd tried to convince her mother to come as well, even offering to buy lunch for everyone at The Grill, but Barbie was morose and wouldn't be budged. Aubrey knew the source of her mother's mood—Barbie had been quite vocal earlier that morning—but there was little she could do about her father's continued silence when it came to his wife. She did wonder why Barbie couldn't at least see where her husband's anger came from instead of alternately railing at him via voice mail for his decisions and pleading with him to call her back. It was quite heartbreaking, in a pathetic sort of way, yet Aubrey felt removed from it all. The sad thing was, Barbie had alienated her years ago. The sting of it had finally faded and Aubrey wasn't interested in going back.

But for her sister she couldn't help but feel compelled to reach out to her. It was that twin thing, she knew, but it didn't change the fact that her sister's tears had an effect on her.

"Why did you move here?" Arianna asked as they drove to town. She watched the scenery, brilliant in its fall colors, as they passed it by but Aubrey knew her sister wasn't appreciating the view. "It's nothing like what we're accustomed to."

"That's exactly why I came here," Aubrey admitted. "It's no secret that I didn't fit in with that life. There's a rhythm here that I recognize and identify with. Plus…I needed somewhere to be while I dealt with…" She sighed, even hating mentioning her ex's name. "Well, you know what happened with Derek."

Arianna nodded absently. "You do have a talent for bringing home stray dogs," she noted, pricking Aubrey's tender feelings.

"Thanks," she said, offended. "You're not much better in that department. As I recall your last boyfriend cheated on you with your supposed best friend."

"That was embarrassing," Arianna agreed, frowning slightly. "He could've been a little more discreet. But I wouldn't exactly say I was in love with him or anything, so who cares?"

"You were engaged. You must've felt something for him," she reminded her sister.

Arianna shrugged. "The equivalent of an arranged marriage. Frankly, I'm not even sure why I broke it off with him. It would've been a good match and he had political aspirations so who knows where we might've landed in a decade or two. I rather like the idea of being a First Lady. Has a nice ring. The fact is, I probably just succumbed to a PMS moment. If I'd been thinking rationally…I'd probably be married by now. Our wedding was going to be spectacular. The party of the season. Did you know I had ordered exotic flowers from Hawaii? Gorgeous. Besides, who's ever faithful anymore? It's such an outdated concept in this day and age."

"Stop it," Aubrey demanded, hating this apathetic version of her sister who had taken over since the news of their financial situation had dropped. "What is wrong with you? It's okay to feel something. You broke it off with Nicholas because he was a two-timing pig who was sleeping with everything that moved. You broke up with him because you deserve better."

Arianna's mouth twitched. "My little champion. Always looking for the noble cause. I'd have thought after Derek you might've given that up. The fact is, Aubrey, monogamy is so provincial. Discretion is what's respected these days."

"I'm not afraid to admit that I loved Derek and I loved his kids," Aubrey said, a phantom pain blossoming in her chest at the thought of the children—not the man—she no longer had the privilege to care about. "You can admit that you cared about Nicholas and you were hurt by his actions."

"Whatever helps you get through the day." Arianna looked away. "It doesn't matter. I'm no longer a suitable wife for anyone in our former circle."

"Oh, Arianna, listen to yourself. You used to have fire

and spunk and you could give a crap about those stupid, shallow idiots who ran around with Mother and Daddy. Now, you're letting their useless ideals shape your self-worth. Frankly, I think this situation with Daddy has been a blessing in disguise. Now you can find out who your true friends are and weed out the excess baggage weighing you down. You don't want a man who's going to determine your worth by your social standing or the houses you own or the vacation spots you visit on the off-season."

"Aubrey...spare me. The only reason you're not devastated by this new development is because you're sitting pretty on a nice chunk of change. You don't have to find a job, you work because you want to. I don't have that option. I'm *broke*. So please spare me your self-righteous speeches. I can't even hop a plane out of this godforsaken place because my credit card has been canceled. I can't even go to the grocery store to buy food. But that's not the case for you. You have enough money squirreled away to suit your needs just fine. So *bravo*, Aubrey, for being your uptight, penny-pinching self. It has served you well."

Aubrey gaped, knowing with a certainty that her sister had snooped through her financial paperwork. The knowledge both angered her for Arianna's disregard for her privacy and made her feel slightly ashamed for taking such a high road when her sister was right. Over the years she'd invested wisely the money her father gave her in allowance, preferring to live by what she made in her paycheck and, no, she wasn't in danger of starving any time soon. But that didn't give her sister the right to snoop. In the face of that scathing statement, Aubrey made a stiff request. "I'd appreciate if you'd stay out of my financial paperwork while you are a *guest* in my home. My finances are my business. Not yours."

"No problem, sister-mine. I've already seen what I needed to see. And for the record, I think it's disgusting that you would withhold money from your family. It would seem you and Daddy are definitely cut from the same cloth."

"As you and Mother certainly are, as well," Aubrey muttered, sending her sister a dark look, but Arianna had already returned her attention to the scenery, which suited Aubrey fine. It took every ounce of self-control she possessed not to toss Arianna out on her ear. In the state of mind she was in, she didn't even think she'd slow down before giving her the boot.

CHAPTER NINE

IT WAS TWO DAYS AFTER her and Arianna's big blowup that Aubrey's father finally called.

"Daddy? Where are you? What's going on? Phil says we're broke. Is that true?"

The line was scratchy, which told Aubrey wherever her father was wasn't close—perhaps not even in the same country—and her heart sank. "Hello, darling," her father said brightly, surprising her with his cheerfulness. "How are you holding up?"

"Fine, Daddy, but Mother and Arianna aren't doing so well. When are you going to talk with Mother?"

Her father sighed deeply and she could almost picture his perplexed expression; it was one he'd worn often. "I suppose we'll talk soon enough. I have paperwork that will arrive by courier. Phil was kind enough to procure your address for the lawyers."

"Lawyers?" she repeated, dread making her voice thin. "Daddy...why do you need lawyers?"

"Oh, honey...it's not been working for a long time and I'm through cleaning up her messes. Time for her to stand on her own two feet and make her own way."

"Are you talking about Mother or Arianna?" she asked.

"Both. But mainly your mother. Aubrey...I'm asking for a divorce."

Tears sprung to Aubrey's eyes and she had to blink hard to send them scurrying, but she gripped the phone tighter. "Daddy, think about what you're doing. This isn't a decision you should make when you're angry." She tried appealing to his sense of logic, but when he chuckled she felt her hopes spiral. "You've been thinking of this for a long time, haven't you?"

"Longer than you realize," he admitted. "The truth is...I'm ready to be happy and I've found someone who shares the same ideals as me."

The bottom of Aubrey's world dropped open. "You're seeing someone? Already?" She couldn't keep the accusation from her voice. "Daddy, what's gotten into you?"

"I've finally come to my senses," he said gruffly. "And it's not your decision to make so don't sit there and judge me. I expected more from you."

Her heart beat painfully but she couldn't succumb just yet; she needed to know what was going to happen. It was not lost on her that her father was dumping the responsibility of his wife and other daughter squarely in her lap so that he could be *happy* elsewhere. It belied what she thought she knew of her father and that hurt more than his defection. "Phil says we're broke. Is that true?" she asked tightly.

Her father made a small noise that sounded like stalling and she prompted him again. "Daddy...I need to know."

"The lawyers will hash everything out, darling. Just remember I love you and always will. When this is all settled and tempers have calmed down, we'll get together and have lunch. I truly think you'll like Fiona once you get to know her."

The line went dead and it was several long minutes before Aubrey could breathe again without wanting to scream. Her mother was going to...*freak*.

And honestly, Aubrey couldn't find it in her heart to blame her. Harold Rose had done a number on them all.

SAMMY FOUND HIS MOTHER in the attic, rummaging through boxes. His first view when he poked his head through the trapdoor was of Mary's stout behind bobbing up and down as she hummed and bounced to her own tune. He stifled a laugh and cleared his throat. "Ma...you busy?" he asked, startling her as she whirled around to see who was at her backside.

"Lend me a hand, will you?" she asked, without missing a beat, gesturing to the box she was standing over. "Your father and I have decided to take up line dancing again and I want to find my cowboy boots. I know I put them up here somewhere," she muttered. "But darn if all these boxes don't look alike."

Sammy hauled the box into a better position so his mother could rip into it, and decided there was no time better than the present to do a little snooping of his own.

"So...how well do you know Aubrey?" he asked.

Mary shrugged without slowing her search. "I don't really."

"So how did you know whether or not she was a good candidate for a nanny?"

"I didn't. What's with all the questions? Something wrong?" she asked, straightening for a moment to regard him with a frown. "Aubrey hasn't done something to Ian, has she?"

"No, not at all. I'm just getting to know her a little better and wondered what you knew about her. I mean, she's not from around here. You're usually pretty reserved when it comes to outsiders but you practically threw her into my lap when it came time to get Ian a nanny."

She scowled. "I did not throw her at you, Samuel. You make it sound as if I'm some tyrant." Sammy bit back a grin and she sniffed at his attempt at holding back laughter. "I'm assertive…there's a difference," she clarified before continuing. "I confess I don't know much about her but my gut told me she would be a good fit. Sort of how I knew Annabelle would be a good fit for your brother."

"Whoa now, Ma, we're talking nanny not nuptials."

This time Mary grinned. "Of course."

But it was that grin that gave Sammy the willies. "C'mon, Ma, you gotta promise no matchmaking. I'm not interested in starting a romance with her or anyone else," he warned.

She arched a thin eyebrow. "Oh? That's not how I'm hearing it around town. Seems you've been doing a lot of *romancing* lately. Unless my sources are deluded and it's not you out nearly every night tearing things up, looking for trouble or an easy tumble."

His ears burned to hear his mother talk about his sex life. "All right, but it ain't romance and you and I know it. What I had with Dana…I'm not likely to find with someone else." *Least of all with his nanny.* "Nor am I interested in looking for it."

"No one is saying you are," she replied.

"Good. Just want to make sure we're clear."

"Of course, son."

And even though her words sounded sincere, the sense that she was just humoring him and fully intended to proceed with her own agenda wouldn't quit. "Ma…" he warned and she shooed him away.

"If you're just going to give me a hard time, you can get on with yourself. I have boots to find. If you're going to be helpful, then roll up your sleeves and start opening these boxes. I aim to find those boots before dark." She paused, taking a good look at his fading bruises and smiled knowingly. "Mouth overload your ass again?" she asked, vastly amused.

"You could say that," he said with a growl. "Or maybe your other sons haven't quite accepted that they don't run my life."

"Nope. I'd say it's the former," she announced smugly. "So what's it going to be? Help or not? Make up your mind, the sun ain't waiting on either of us."

Sammy scratched at his head, knowing there was no

way in hell he was going to be able to walk out of his mother's house without lending a hand—he just wasn't raised that way—so he rolled up his sleeves and started pulling boxes.

"You're a good boy, Samuel Halvorsen," his mother said.

He grunted. "If you say so, Ma."

"I do. Now get to work."

AUBREY DIDN'T KNOW HOW TO approach her mother and sister about her conversation with Harold, so she kept it quiet until she could figure something out. In the meantime, she felt tense all over from the pressure of having to deliver such damaging news and anger at her entire family for the whole mess.

Her relationship with Arianna had become worse than ever before. Aside from the stilted and abrupt conversation over breakfast, there was little else between them, and time spent with her mother was painful.

Never before had she seen her mother so dejected. She hated that Barbie suspected what was coming down the pipe yet it didn't make the delivery any easier.

"Mother, have you reconsidered joining the Quilters Brigade?" she asked over a hastily eaten bagel before she headed to work. Usually so meticulous in her appearance, Barbie was beginning to look each and every one of her fifty-six years, and considering how much money she'd spent to avoid that very thing, it was a travesty for dollar value alone. Add the grief that was etching itself plainly onto her skin with each passing day, and Aubrey couldn't help but worry. "I think it would do you good to get your mind off things."

"Honestly, Aubrey," Barbie said dispiritedly as she raised her coffee mug to her lips. "I have not sunk that low yet."

I beg to differ, she wanted to retort but held her tongue. "I'm just saying it might help to get to know a new circle of friends while you're here."

"Your father will come to his senses soon. He's punishing me but he'll come around. He always does. Your father is trying to teach me a lesson. But this will all blow over soon. I just need to be patient. Likely, he's going to surprise me with some jewelry when he's calmed down. I hope it's diamonds and not emeralds. Green has never agreed with my skin tone."

There were no such gifts coming Barbie's way this time. And a part of her thought her mother knew this but just couldn't acknowledge it out loud because that would make the situation real. Aubrey swallowed the sudden lump in her throat and her mouth sealed shut to prevent the truth from spilling out. She couldn't tell her just yet. Barbie was likely to try and off herself with the shower curtain.

"Just give it some thought," Aubrey suggested and hurried out the door before her guilt got the best of her.

AUBREY CAME THROUGH THE DOOR, her expression tense and distracted, and rushed past Sammy as she prepared

Ian's breakfast. "I'm sorry I'm a little late," she said, moving about the kitchen with brisk efficiency. Funny how she'd become a fixture in his house in a relatively short time, he mused as she made fast work of Ian's favorite rice cereal mixture. He tried not to grimace. It looked like Spackle to him but the kid sure ate it up like it was chocolate mousse, so that's all that mattered.

"It's okay. Everything good?" he asked.

She risked a quick look but then returned to her task. "Fine," she answered. "Just running behind."

He didn't know her well but he was willing to hazard a guess that everything was not fine. That whatever was biting her in the butt was clamped down hard but she sure wasn't going to share with him and he didn't blame her for her reservation. But...call it curiosity, call it nosiness, he couldn't resist the pull of wanting to know what was wrong. "I'm a pretty good listener," he offered with a twist of his lips. "At least, that's what I've been told."

She met his gaze, those brown eyes—beautiful and dark, edgy and sort of mysterious—staring him down. "You'll get no pillow talk from me, Mr. Halvorsen. Don't you have a job to get to? Please don't let me hold you up."

And that, folks, is why you don't tangle with your boy's nanny, a voice inside his head chided. "Coffee is in the pot. Help yourself," he said, moving away from the counter where he'd been leaning. "Have a good day, Ms. Rose."

He was nearly to the door when her voice cut into him with its edge. "Would it kill you to show your son some affection?" she asked tightly. The minute it came out of her mouth he could tell she was appalled that she'd said it out loud. He had no doubt she said all sorts of things inside that head of hers but it surprised him— probably as much as it surprised her—that she'd let it slip. Seeing as she'd already opened her mouth, she continued, "I'm just saying, it has not escaped my notice that you never offer Ian any sign that you care for him. Those things matter to a child. Were you raised in a household where no one hugged or kissed?"

Nope. Exact opposite. His ma hadn't been stingy in that department; his father, neither, though he had a different style of showing his affection. But Sammy had never felt slighted. He held her glare, momentarily mesmerized by the way her eyes darkened with the force of her anger, and then shook it off for the pure lunacy it was and countered without exactly answering. "Were you?"

"As a matter of fact, I was. And I can tell you, it wasn't pleasant," she admitted after a short standoff of sorts. "And if you weren't raised that way then why are you doing it to your son?"

He stiffened, all hints of jocularity or friendliness fleeing from his voice as he said, "You are my nanny, not my therapist. Let's keep that clear."

"Fine by me," she said, her mouth tightening. "Have a good day."

And then he was dismissed. Damn, how'd that happen? There was a cultured and refined lilt to her voice that managed to make him feel as if he'd just been the one to trespass and she was—without saying much—

reprimanding him. *Women*. Their talents were bound-less, he wanted to mutter as he slammed out the door.

AUBREY WAS FUMING BUT SHE tried to tamp it down for Ian's sake. The baby was already frowning and on the verge of tears when Sammy startled him with the slamming front door. Didn't the man realize what he was doing to his son? Of course not. He was too busy thinking of himself to take notice of anyone else, least of all the one person who was too small to give him a piece of his mind.

She gave Ian an extra squeeze and he giggled, content to grasp at her hair for a quick tug and she responded with a tummy blow that made him laugh harder. Ian's eyes lit up like a summer day and his cheeks were plump and rosy, almost too pretty for a boy. She cocked her head at Ian. "You must stop being so adorable right this very instance," she said in a mock-stern voice, which only made Ian purse his lips and blow a spit bubble.

Laughing, she wiped his mouth and plopped him into his baby seat for his breakfast. She was just finishing when there was a knock at the door. Wiping her hands free of the rice cereal that always managed to jump from the spoon to her fingers no matter how hard she tried to keep it where it belonged, she plucked Ian from his seat and went to the door.

Staring back at her was a woman who could be her twin, except she wasn't Arianna.

"Damn...we do look alike," the woman said then

thrust her hand forward to grab Aubrey in a firm handshake as if they were men. "Name's Nora Simmons-Hollister—a mouthful I know but I'm a modern woman and I said he could give up his name or I could hyphenate mine, and well, he wasn't keen on giving up his name so I have a name long enough to choke a horse—" She drew a deep breath and continued, "I figure we might as well get this out of the way because it's going to happen eventually."

"What's going to happen?" Aubrey asked, uncertain and not quite sure what to think of the bold blonde regarding her shrewdly.

"I'm Sammy's best friend, have been since…I can't remember honestly and I wanted to see for myself what everyone's been talking about."

"Who's talking about what?" she asked, gesturing so Nora could come in.

Nora waved away her concern. "Small-town stuff. Can't pee without someone wanting to know the color. The thing is Sammy's been partying like it's going out of style and then you come along and it's got people talking. I mean, are you gunning to be the next Mrs Sammy Halvorsen? Because if you are I have to tell you that's an exercise in futility and you ought to save your energy for something more worthwhile."

Horrified at the thought, she gaped at this strange woman. She let her revulsion show as she adjusted Ian on her hip. "Why would *anyone* want to be saddled to that nitwit?" Aubrey asked in disgust. "He's inconsid-

erate, rude and impatient. I can't imagine a more un-
suitable husband unless you were a baboon who spent
more time scratching at yourself than paying attention
to what your partner is doing."

She half expected Nora to puff up and start yelling at
her for insulting Sammy, but Nora surprised her with a
hearty laugh. "You've got spunk. Good. You'll need it in
this town. Let's sit down and chat. I only have a short
window until I have to pick up Jackson—that's my son—
from my dad's and I want to get to know you better."

Aubrey risked a small smile, wondering what would
spill from Nora. Aubrey was always willing to glean
more information about her taciturn employer from
those in his personal circle. Oh sure, she could ask him
these things herself but she had a feeling this woman—
who was helping herself to a cup of coffee as if she
owned the place—wouldn't hold back or mince words
and that was a refreshing thought.

"So you don't like Sammy, huh?" Nora asked,
settling into the sofa and tucking her feet under her. "I
don't blame you. I don't much like him these days,
either. Can't say anyone does. Right now he's quite the
horse's ass."

Aubrey laughed. "You can say that again. Are you
saying there's another side to him that I haven't seen?"

Nora sipped her coffee. "Oh, yeah. Believe it or not,
Sammy is a crack-up under normal circumstances.
He's the guy who's the life of the party, the comedian,
the charming little hottie at the bar who's winking at

you in one breath and slipping you his phone number in the other."

"Well, I've seen him try his Rico Sauve number but it fell pretty flat on me so if that was his top game…he struck out big-time."

"Sounds like what happened with Dana. I think that was part of her charm at first. She was totally turned off by his act. He's out of his element when faced with rejection."

Aubrey settled in, delighted to be getting firsthand information. It was completely gossipy and Aubrey was eating it up. "Were you friends with Dana, too?"

A frown settled on Nora's face, piquing Aubrey's interest considerably. "Yeah, not really. I mean, we got along because we had to. Sammy was my best friend, and she was his wife. We were friendly but not friends, you know what I mean?"

Sort of like Aubrey with her sister at times. Aubrey nodded. "Yeah, I get it. I probably sound terrible when I say I'm glad to hear that not everyone was in love with Dana. Don't get me wrong, I have nothing against her, I just can't believe that anyone is that good."

"No one is perfect and she certainly wasn't," Nora said drily but then quickly added. "But she wasn't bad, either. Sometimes, well, most of the time, I was the difficult one. I should be honest with you…"

"No explanations necessary," Aubrey said with a smile. She liked Nora. "Not everyone is meant to get along with everyone else. I don't get along with my sister most of the time. She's my twin and I think in spite of identical genes…we're cut from two different bolts of cloth."

"Sounds like me and my sister Natalie. We're as different as they come. I used to wonder if she was switched at birth because she's nothing like me or my other sister."

"Is your sister Tasha?"

"Yeah…you know her?"

"Only slightly. She was at the Quilters Brigade meeting the other night with Annabelle and Mary Halvorsen. I didn't see you there, though."

"Hell no and you never will. Quilting is the equivalent of the Chinese water torture when I'm involved. I'm a terrible student. I much prefer Bingo or spending *quality*—" she waggled her eyebrows "—time with my husband. Besides, Tasha has the patience of a saint having spent so much time in the Peace Corps when she was in her early twenties. She can handle all that quilting stuff without blinking an eye. Not me."

Aubrey laughed and blushed just a little. God, it'd been so long since she'd had sex…she barely remembered what it was like. Had it been good with Derek? It must've been. Yet, she couldn't recall any toe-curling memories…more like pleasant tingles that were nice but certainly not earthshaking. A frown formed before she could stop it and Nora misinterpreted the gesture and quickly apologized.

"Ben's always telling me I should think first before talking but that's usually about the same time I tell him to pound sand and make himself useful in the kitchen or the bedroom and all that good advice goes right out the window." She snickered. "I'm just kidding. I don't really boss my husband around like that but it's fun to try. He's right, though, and I try to think before I speak these days but... I'm sorry if I said something inappropriate."

"Please don't censor yourself on my account. I've spent my entire life around people who never said how they felt or believed what they said, so please, say what you want. It's refreshing."

"That's a first," Nora acknowledged with a toothy grin. "Most times people are giving me *that look* that says *I can't believe she just said that.* I'm used to it by now but it's nice to know that you're not easily shocked. Perhaps I've finally found my partner in crime."

"Perhaps you have." Aubrey smiled. There was a companionable silence until Nora said, "So, now that we've broken the ice, why don't you tell me how Mary managed to rope you into this deal?"

"I love kids. I wasn't that hard to convince," Aubrey murmured with a warm glance directed at Ian, who was playing with his toys on the floor. "And how could I say no to that adorable little face? He's gotta be the cutest kid on the planet."

"He's pretty cute, even though he's the spitting image of Dana," Nora agreed with a nod, then sighed. "I think it'd be easier for Sammy if he'd looked more like him instead."

Aubrey was silent for a moment. "It's not fair for

Sammy to take out his grief on Ian just because his son bears an uncanny resemblance to his dead wife."

"You're right, but it doesn't change the fact that Sammy can hardly bear to be around him for that same reason."

Aubrey gaped at Nora. "That's why he's so distant with Ian?"

Nora shrugged. "Well, it's not like we had a sit-down and chatted about it but that would be my guess. Besides, it's obvious. Don't you think?"

Aubrey considered this and decided Nora was right. But that didn't make it okay. In fact, it just made her angrier with him for his selfishness. Nora must've read her expression, for she grinned and said, "Getting mad is good. He needs a swift kick in the butt. If I wasn't so busy with my own kid and husband I'd do you the favor but my days of kicking his sorry rear around have come to an end. Perhaps you'd like to do it for a while?"

Aubrey lost some of her ire in the face of Nora's easy way even as she declined with a chuckle. "Sorry. I have enough of my own troubles to deal with. Sammy will just have to shape up on his own. I'm through trying to save other people when they can grab the rope for themselves."

"Amen to that. Although to be fair, I've never been in much of a habit of saving others, either. Sink or swim or get out of my way is my motto."

"It sounds like a damn good one," Aubrey agreed.

Yes, she liked Nora. Perhaps more than she liked anyone aside from Ian at that moment. And that included her own family.

CHAPTER TEN

SAMMY WAS KNOCKING BACK A BEER at Gilly's Friday night when he noticed everyone around him suddenly turned to stare at who was walking in the door. Small-town bars were worse than sixth-grade classrooms—the attention spans were nearly as short as the skirts but if anyone new came in everyone had to take a gander.

He swiveled in his chair and did a double take. Aubrey? Wait. It looked like Aubrey—shit, it looked a lot like Aubrey—but there was something about the way the woman handled herself, aloof and with a somewhat angry gaze as she swept the room before settling at the bar beside him, that made her different.

She appraised him openly, her hard gaze softening ever so slightly as she clearly appreciated what she saw, then said, "Buy a girl a drink?"

"Sure," he said slowly, gesturing to the barkeep, yet wondered at her game. When she left today she hadn't said anything about going out on the town. Not that she had to give him an itinerary on her comings and goings but…he surely hadn't expected to see her walk through Gilly's doors. And certainly not dressed like that.

Since turnabout was fair play, he let his gaze wander. The tight jeans hugged her backside and rode low on her hips so that if she leaned forward just a little, he'd get a sneak peak at her thong. His face flushed at the thought, and he tried pulling his X-rated mind away from the enticing image and focused on his beer. But even through his tipped mug his eyeballs zeroed right in on the tempting show of plump cleavage that dared him to cross barriers, throw his good sense out the window and pull out all the stops to seduce his nanny. He downed his beer and signaled for another even though he had a feeling he ought to just pay the tab and go home. Dean and Annabelle had Ian so it wasn't like he had anyone to go home to but…what was going round in his head smacked of a terrible idea, one that was likely to spell really bad consequences.

"Who's watching the kid?" she asked, her tongue darting out to moisten her lips. His groin tightened and he shifted inconspicuously on the stool.

"Dean and Annabelle," he answered. Funny, Aubrey never called Ian *the kid*. That was something he did and he was pretty sure she hated it. "What's gotten into you?" he blurted out. So much for finesse.

Her gaze narrowed. "What do you mean? A girl can't enjoy a drink every now and again?"

"Don't get huffy. I'm just saying you're acting different. I've never seen you like this," he said.

"Like what exactly?" she asked innocently, giving him a sultry look that nearly fried his brain cells, yet there was something off about the whole thing, too. Aubrey wasn't the kind of woman who… Actually, he didn't know her well enough to assume he knew her at all. Maybe she was the kind of person who led a double life and spent her days being a mild-mannered, prim and nearly painfully proper nanny but by night she was a whip-wielding dominatrix. He eyed the woman before him speculatively but couldn't reconcile that image in his head even though she looked pretty damn dangerous right about now.

"I like to have fun," she said with a hint of a smile, revealing the tips of her pearly teeth, teasing him with the coy look in her eye. "Don't you? I've heard stories…. I guess I'm curious about Sammy Halvorsen…."

She let her voice trail and he felt himself being pulled in her direction like a magnet was buried inside his forehead and he was just doing what nature intended. There was something hypnotic about the slick sheen of her lips that beckoned, and well, she was hot.

He felt his pulse quicken even though somehow it felt all wrong, and finally, giving in to his baser, more primal instinct, he sealed the distance and took what she offered.

Hot damn. Holy crap. Somehow…he knew he wasn't kissing Aubrey.

And it wasn't because Aubrey—the real Aubrey— was heading right for him and she was *pissed.* Everything up until that moment had been off but it wasn't until he was in a lip-lock with her that he realized she didn't *smell* like Aubrey.

SOMEHOW NORA HAD CONVINCED Aubrey to hit the town for a drink. She'd relented only because the thought of watching her mother's continued spiral into a deep depression was not high on her list—particularly when Aubrey's guilt for her cowardly silence only made it worse—and Nora had this infectious way about her that Aubrey was only too happy to indulge.

But the promise of good times died the moment she entered the bar, the laughter tickling her lips only a heartbeat earlier dwindling to a horrified gasp, when she saw Sammy Halvorsen belly up to the bar in a disgusting, open-mouthed kiss with none other than...*her sister*.

Nora gaped and stared wide-eyed while Aubrey felt her temperature hit the boiling point as Sammy jerked away from Arianna as if he'd been burned, the look of confusion clear on his face but Aubrey was too angry to care.

Arianna, of course, found the whole situation quite comical in a rich-bitch-I'm-amused-by-the-humiliation-of-others sort of way and laughed. "Gotcha," she said to Sammy. "We used to pull the twin switcheroo all the time. I was feeling nostalgic, I guess."

Aubrey speared Sammy with a black look that promised retribution but turned on her sister, ready to become one less twin. "I said you could borrow my car. I didn't say you could pretend to be me and slobber all over my employer," she said in a low voice that trembled with her rage. "You've gone too far and you know it."

Arianna slid to her feet and gave Aubrey an insolent look that went quite well with the sneer in her voice as she said, "You're not *my* nanny. So do me a favor and go away. I'm here to have some fun. And if Sammy is game, so am I. A girl could die from boredom in this hick town but at least I could die with a smile on my face."

"How did you even know who he was?" Aubrey demanded.

Arianna gave Aubrey a bored look. "The only good thing about small towns is how easy it is to find someone, especially someone related to the town's founder. He was pathetically easy to find." She turned and sent Sammy a wink. "If I were an assassin, you'd be a dead man."

Aubrey was so angry all she could do was fume as Arianna sauntered off, swiveling her hips in a way that alternately embarrassed Aubrey for the display and horrified her that people may have mistaken Arianna for her.

Sammy looked sheepish and mortified for what just happened and if she hadn't been roiling with every type of negative emotion known to man, she might've dredged up a little sympathy. They were identical but there were subtle differences and if he'd known her at all he would've caught on to those quite easily.

"I don't know what to say," Sammy started but was cut off by Nora's laughter. He glared but she simply blew him a kiss and left him and Aubrey to deal with one another in private. He lifted his hands and then shoved them in his pocket. "I forgot you had a twin," he said.

"You forgot?" she repeated incredulously. What a lame statement in light of the situation. "So what are you saying? That you truly thought it was me and you thought I wanted to have a little fun?" He gave her a helpless little shrug that told her that's exactly what he'd thought and her cheeks started to burn. "I've been your nanny for two months! You can't tell the difference between me and…someone else?"

"You're identical!" he protested, a dark frown gathering on his brow when she simply shook her head. "You could've at least warned me that there's another one of you running around. And since when is your sister in town?"

She crossed her arms. "I didn't realize I was required to give you an itinerary on the comings and goings of my family. So sorry for not getting that memo. News flash—my mother and sister are in town. Would you like to go feel up my mom now?"

"That's going too far," he said with a glower.

"Really? Because from where I'm standing it seems quite appropriate." She tapped a finger to her lips and glared. "Oh, wait, perhaps I should've left you a note stating as such so that in the event you're feeling horny and alone you don't stick your tongue down my sister's throat."

"What is your problem?" he shouted, drawing attention from the other bar patrons. He lowered his voice but the intensity remained. "We're not dating. We're not *anything*. So if I wanted to stick my tongue down your sister's throat as you call it, there's nothing that says I couldn't if she were so inclined. Frankly, I think I like your sister better. She's not as *uptight* or *self-righteous*. You on the other hand wouldn't know how to have fun if it were written in a manual." He fished a wad of cash out of his pocket and tossed it to the bar with a sneer. "Here. Have a drink on me. You need it."

And then he stalked out, pushing both doors open with such force that they banged against the walls, eliciting a shout of warning from the bouncer. Sammy made a gesture that said *yeah, whatever* and then he was gone.

SAMMY SLAMMED HIS TRUCK DOOR shut and gunned the engine, not quite sure why he was so fired up. He felt as if he'd done something terribly wrong. He imagined this is what it might feel like if he'd cheated on his wife. He felt dirty and lower than pond scum and pissed off for feeling that way because he was innocent.

And what the hell kind of game was Aubrey's sister playing? Clearly, she'd realized that he thought she was Aubrey and had had fun at his expense. Twins. He had no one to blame but himself for not remembering that Aubrey was a twin. Like the world needed another Aubrey Rose. He didn't even know her sister's name. Damn, he'd been played. How often did that happen? All of about—hmm, never. Sure it sucked and it was humiliating but what really bit him in the ass about the whole thing was…he'd *wanted* to kiss Aubrey. He'd *thought* he was kissing Aubrey. So where'd that leave him? Confused. Irritated. And oddly tuned up, tense as a bowstring, wishing he could walk back into that bar and grab the real Aubrey to rectify the situation.

Her sister had been hot but Aubrey—the real deal—had been sexy as hell. Especially when the fire had lit up her eyes. If he'd been made of paper, he'd have been a pile of ash. What was wrong with him? He didn't want a woman with a temper—someone who was territorial and possessive—he wanted easy, complacent…a good-time girl who liked a good tumble and didn't stick around for too much cuddle time afterward. Quick and dirty was fine with him, so was long and sweaty, but in the end, he wanted no attachments. He couldn't have that with Aubrey. She'd never even consider a quick fling with him and he knew that for a certainty even if he knew nothing more.

And he realized he respected that about her. It reminded him of someone else and his heart contracted painfully. Dana had been like that. Solid, chock-full of integrity and values in spite of her rough upbringing. He'd loved that about her. Sammy inhaled a sharp breath and let it out slowly as the grief he carried with him on a daily basis intensified.

Aubrey…was so off-limits. No matter what. His heart could only take so much. And he'd just about reached that mark.

CHAPTER ELEVEN

AUBREY STARED AFTER SAMMY as he stalked from the bar, her anger mixing with surprise at his reaction.

Nora thrust a beer into Aubrey's hand, which she accepted as if she were on autopilot but continued to gape in the direction Sammy had left. "How dare he say that I'm uptight," she said, stung.

"He's just embarrassed to be caught macking on your sister. To be fair, I think that would knock anyone for a loop. Here, bottom's up. Sammy's buying so we might as well take advantage of it," Nora said, tipping her beer for a good swallow.

Aubrey regarded the beer bottle in her hand and then, after a moment's hesitation, took a drink, as well. "I know how to have fun," she said darkly, earning a peal of laughter from Nora. "I do!"

"Of course you do. I have a sixth sense about people and I knew the moment I saw you that you were going to be entertaining. Now, drink up so we can hit the dance floor. It's been a long time since I had another woman I could go out dancing with and my feet are itching to move."

"I'm not going out there with Arianna," Aubrey said, glowering. "There's no telling what I might do to her."

"Forget her. Don't let her attitude ruin our night," Nora said easily. "One thing's for certain, she'll always be your sister so you can only stay angry for so long. Just ignore her until she comes to her senses."

"Hell might freeze over before that happens. Arianna's the antithesis of rational." *Especially now,* she wanted to add under her breath but didn't because she didn't feel up to explaining. "But you're right. I shouldn't let her ruin everything," she agreed, lifting her beer in salute to Nora's good advice. "Bottom's up."

"Atta girl," Nora cheered and took a swig, too. "Now let's see if you can shake what your mama gave you. This is my favorite song!"

Aubrey had just enough time to swallow what was in her mouth before Nora was pulling her onto the crowded dance floor with a whoop and a holler.

Before long, she completely forgot how angry she was with her sister and Sammy, and by her estimation, that was a good thing because Aubrey was fairly certain there might've been bloodshed.

BY MONDAY MORNING, Aubrey had lost her feel-good vibes from the dancing on Friday night and she felt the anger simmering just beneath the surface at both her sister and Sammy. To make matters worse, living conditions in her house had become downright impossible. She'd tried to draw her mother out of the house on some errands, just to give her a change of scenery, but Barbie had stubbornly refused, preferring to remain at the house. Aubrey knew why she didn't want to leave the house and the knowledge pained her. But Aubrey didn't press—even though her conscience told her otherwise—and went on her errands alone. Arianna, wisely, avoided her. But even so, Aubrey was very distressed to find her formerly happy cottage had been contaminated with the sad and dour energy of her family.

And then there was the issue of Sammy to deal with and that's exactly what she was going to do, she decided, as she walked into the house, removing her scarf and hanging it on the jacket hook. As she was about to announce her arrival, she realized Sammy was trying to feed Ian his breakfast, except Ian looked ready to bawl, his face was puckering, and he kept avoiding the spoon in spite of Sammy's insistence that he eat. Curious, she hung back a minute to see what Sammy would do.

"You eat it up with Aubrey. C'mon, it's good," he said, though his tone said the exact opposite. Ian turned away and whimpered. "It can't be that bad." Sammy took an exploratory bite and grimaced as he forced it down. "What is this crap?" he muttered, lifting the bowl to sniff it. "The box said rice cereal but I'm pretty sure this is shower caulking in disguise."

Aubrey hid a smile.

Sammy tried one more time to get Ian to eat and Ian reacted by swatting at the spoon, which went flying out of Sammy's fingers. Rice cereal, bowl and spoon toppled to the floor with a loud clatter.

"Son of a—"

"Good morning," Aubrey cut in, surprising Sammy with her sudden appearance. "Someone's made a mess," she observed, watching as Sammy jerked a few paper towels from the roll.

"Yeah. You noticed."

"Why didn't you just wait for me?"

He finished wiping up the mess and threw the towels away. His movements were short and tense. "The kid was hungry," he said by way of explanation. "I was tired of hearing him cry."

Aubrey's first reaction was to snap that perhaps if he'd paid attention to how his son liked his cereal the baby would've enjoyed it but then she realized, or maybe she just hoped, that Sammy had been trying in some small way to reach out to his son and she tempered her tongue.

Sammy started to stalk from the room, muttering about the whole experience, and Aubrey called out to him. He stopped and reluctantly turned.

"The secret is apple juice," she said. To his look of confusion, she grabbed the box of cereal. "He likes it made with apple juice...not water. Gives it some flavor."

Dawning broke in his expression and he gave a curt nod, though there was something about his eyes that appeared bleak and defeated that tugged at her.

"Keep trying," she said in an attempt to lift his spirits. "You'll get the hang of it."

Sammy remained silent and then shook his head. "I'm going to be late."

And then he was gone.

Aubrey sighed and looked at Ian. "I think he's trying. Cut him some slack, okay, little guy?"

Ian blew a raspberry and then grinned for his accomplishment. She ruffled his hair softly. "I know…it's a work in progress."

SAMMY'S FOUL MOOD RODE HIM all the way into town. He felt like an idiot for trying to play daddy when he was plainly not equipped to even feed the kid his breakfast.

But Ian had woken up early and had started fussing. He wanted his breakfast and Sammy didn't blame him. When he woke up he was usually starving, too, so it served to reason his kid might have the same digestion.

He rubbed his brow to relieve the tension. How could one baby be so complicated? What was going to happen when the kid started walking? Talking? Going to school? He didn't know the first thing about getting to know Ian as a baby; what hope did he have to reach him as he grew older? A sense of hopelessness washed over him and he hoped Dana was not watching him flounder. He couldn't bear the thought that she was looking on with deep disappointment at what a failure he was as a father. She would've been a perfect mother, he thought to himself with a spasm of grief. How could fate be so cruel to her…to him?

To Ian.

SEVERAL DAYS LATER, CEREAL incident forgotten, Aubrey was in good spirits.

"Good morning, sweetie," she crooned to the baby as she picked him up for a quick cuddle. He responded with a delighted gurgle that instantly warmed her heart and she kissed his forehead without thinking. She looked up and started when she noticed Sammy was watching her. She straightened, a defensive comment immediately on her tongue until she realized the look in his eyes was not one of disapproval but yearning. She withheld what she might have said in light of that odd show of emotion but in a heartbeat it was gone, which caused her to question whether she'd seen it at all.

"I don't know if it's appropriate for you to be so openly affectionate with the k—" He stopped when she stiffened. "I mean, Ian. It's bad enough he has to grow up without a mom. I don't want him to get attached to you and then get hurt when you leave."

"Babies need affection," she said, any sense of goodwill evaporating. "And since you aren't inclined to offer him any…that leaves me."

"My family gives him plenty of affection," Sammy said, indignant. "Besides, it's not your place."

Tears rushed to her eyes but she nodded. "If you'd prefer I refrain from giving your son kisses on the forehead I will do so but I will not stop hugging and cuddling. Babies need to be touched in order to socialize properly." She tried not to glare when she said it but she was so hurt inside by his request that she nearly turned on her heel and quit. What kept her silent was the child in her arms who was nestled so perfectly against her chest, as if she'd given birth to him herself, that the idea of leaving him made her heart ache. What he was asking was logical, but it went against what she believed babies needed to thrive. She wouldn't worry if Ian had a father who was openly demonstrative with his love but as far as Aubrey could tell, Sammy had a heart the size of a lima bean.

"I just don't want him to be confused," Sammy said gruffly. She acquiesced with a stiff nod but he didn't seem relieved. If anything he seemed surlier as he thrust a cup of coffee her way. "I might be late tonight. Is that okay?" he asked.

"Fine." She took a sip of coffee, calm on the outside yet seething inside. Was he hooking up with Arianna after work? Something ugly and foreign twisted her heart with mean fingers, and the hand holding her coffee cup nearly betrayed her agitation with a tremble. "Special plans?" she asked, striving for nonchalant yet even to her own ears sounding reedy and high pitched.

He sighed as if reading her mind. "I'm not going off to see your sister," he said.

"I wouldn't care if you were," Aubrey replied with a shrug.

A subtle twist of his lips denoted mild amusement at her bald-faced lie but he didn't call her on it. She grudgingly gave him props for being at least that much of a gentleman but since she still had that awful image of her sister and him in her mind, she figured she was a long way off from forgiving if she couldn't at least forget.

He regarded her over his coffee mug and she had to look away from that intense stare of his that seemed to ignite little sparks inside her stomach and threatened to set her whole body on fire. "You can see whom you please, of course," she said, putting her face into her mug so he couldn't read anything from her expression. "I was just…taken aback is all. I should warn you, though."

"Oh? About what?"

"My sister," she said, lowering her cup to the counter so she could put Ian in his high chair for breakfast. She turned to find him watching her with curiosity. She took a deep breath then said, "She's going through a personal crisis and she's not thinking clearly."

His brow furrowed in what looked like concern but somehow Aubrey didn't buy it. "Perhaps she needs a friend. I've been told I'm a good listener," he said mildly.

"Stay away from my sister, you big, fat chowder-head," she said from between gritted teeth before she could stop it.

He surprised her with a hearty laugh and her cheeks burned. "What happened to the 'I don't care who you date' attitude? That changed real quick, didn't it?" he asked, setting his own cup down to study her with a cheeky look in his eyes.

"Fine. You caught me. Bravo. Good detective work. I *loathe* the idea of you dating my sister."

"And why is that?" he asked, some of the mirth

fading from his eyes, replaced with something darker, more intense yet still contained.

"I don't know," she admitted with a shrug. "It just seems wrong." *And weird.* But she didn't say that because it might reveal that she had briefly—nanosecond briefly—wondered why he would kiss Arianna at all if he believed she was Aubrey. Wouldn't that mean he was, at least mildly, attracted to her? And what would *that* mean? Did he consider the possibility of sleeping with her a temporary but pleasant interlude until he moved on to the next warm body or was he looking at her somehow...differently?

He frowned slightly. "You know...it did seem wrong. Off somehow. That's how I knew it wasn't you."

She tried not to be affected by his statement. "Oh? How is that?"

He shrugged. "Subtle difference."

"Which was?" The tiny mole on her cheek? The fact that she was right-handed when Arianna was left? Or how about the fact that Aubrey would never have worn that slutty ensemble in the privacy of her own bedroom much less a crowded bar in a town full of people she hardly knew?

Sammy crossed the small gap between them, startling her as she stared up at him, curious as to what he was going to do, yet painfully aware of every inch of his body so close to her own. She backed away until her behind hit the countertop but he bracketed her body with both arms and leaned forward. "It wasn't until we were about this close," he murmured, his voice tickling the side of her neck as he angled a little closer. She inhaled a sharp breath and her knees threatened to turn to jelly as his mouth hovered near the soft flesh where her neck met her shoulders. The warmth of his lips heated her skin. She could feel his body tantalizingly close and the sensation was nearly as powerful as if he'd pressed against her. "Then I knew it wasn't you."

She swallowed. "What do you mean?"

He inhaled a deep, slow breath as if savoring what he smelled, then said, "Her scent." He pulled away to look into her eyes. "She doesn't smell like you."

"I didn't realize I had a smell," she said, a trifle concerned.

He chuckled softly. "You smell like fresh laundry and lavender. Warm chocolate-chip cookies fresh from the oven. *Delicious.*"

A full-body shudder followed and that was her undoing. She tilted her mouth to his, hungry to taste what he had to offer, eager to feel that body against hers, completely forgetting all the good and sensible reasons why she never again wanted to get involved with the father of the children she was paid to care for. All she wanted at that very moment was to feel Sammy's firm lips taking possession of her own, slanting across her mouth, tongue darting and sliding until she was slick and hot and ready.

But that's not what happened.

Suddenly, Sammy pulled away abruptly and awkwardly patted her on the shoulder like a fishing buddy, saying, "So, yeah, that's how I knew, and well, I gotta go. I'm late for work."

And then he was gone.

Aubrey stared at the closed door and listened to Sammy fire up his truck and rumble down the driveway in shocked silence. But it wasn't long before the shock wore off and was replaced with something else: mortification. And that emotion stayed with her the rest of the day.

IT WAS A HARD DAY FOR SAMMY. Between beating himself up for doing something so damn stupid with Aubrey and desperately wanting to go back and finish the job by jamming his tongue down her throat—eloquent he was not in his current frame of mind—he was a miserable grouch and everyone, including his brothers, gave him a wide berth.

That is until it was quitting time.

Dean headed over with a grin on his face and Sammy knew what was coming. "So I heard Ma wrangled you into taking her line dancing tonight," he said with a chuckle.

Sammy glowered. "Yeah, she said she needs someone to practice with until Dad recovers from his sprained ankle. She doesn't want to get rusty. It's just one class," he barked when Dean burst out laughing.

He clapped Sammy on the shoulder hard enough to leave a bruise but Sammy didn't give his brother the satisfaction of hearing him grunt. "Well, you're a better man than me. She asked me and I begged off saying Annabelle needed me at home tonight."

"She ask Josh, too?"

"Yep. He was smart enough to make something up on the fly, too. That leaves you, little brother, to do-si-do or whatever the hell they do in those kinds of classes. Have fun and don't hurt yourself. Dad said Ma ain't as light on her feet as she used to be."

Sammy swore and rubbed the back of his neck but knew he wouldn't back out. It was his ma and she needed him. Besides, he figured he owed her for putting up with him in the months following Dana's death. He sighed and resigned himself to a night of two-step torture.

CHAPTER TWELVE

AUBREY WAS READING A MAGAZINE when Sammy finally made it home. She'd kept herself busy with Ian, giving him a bath, singing silly songs that made him giggle, and then reading him a book before bed. When Sammy still hadn't shown up, she grabbed a magazine, though she couldn't really say *Car & Driver* was her favorite choice for leisurely reading, but the pictures of hot cars were nice.

Sammy walked in and headed straight for the cabinet where she knew he kept the aspirin. "Sorry I'm late. I didn't expect to be gone so long," he said after tossing back two aspirin and leaning into the sink to wash it down.

"It's fine," Aubrey said, itching to leave. She didn't know how to act around him after the show she'd put on that the morning. A part of her was hoping he'd finish what he started but the other part of her was appalled at the first part and she went around and around until she didn't know what the hell she wanted. "Ian is in bed. He had a bath," she said unnecessarily. Sammy knew she always put him down after a bath. "Annabelle dropped off some fresh milk," she added, silently marveling that it didn't even faze her any longer that Annabelle was bringing breast milk for Ian.

"What? Oh. Good," he mumbled, clearly not as unfazed as Aubrey about the whole thing.

"If it makes you uncomfortable, why do you let her continue?" she asked, unable to help herself.

"It's what Dana would've wanted," he answered roughly. "She was all into that Earth mama stuff. She was even looking into cloth diapers because of the whole disposable diaper/landfill issue. Right before Ian was born I'd finally convinced her to go with the disposable but…she would've wanted Ian to have the best and so…well, you know, breast milk is better and all…" He was beginning to color around the ears, which, oddly, Aubrey found quite endearing.

"So…you're cool with Annabelle expressing breast milk for Ian," she finished for him, enjoying his discomfort. For a supposed ladies' man he was pretty prudish when it came down to basic anatomy. She grinned. "Do you realize when you say *breast* your ears turn red?"

"They do not." He scowled.

"They do. I wouldn't lie about something like that. I would imagine that might crimp your style with the ladies. How do you sweet-talk them with your ears going fire-engine red as if your head's about to catch flame?" she teased.

"When was the last time someone sweet-talked you? I can't remember the last time I used the word *breast* or *breast milk* in my repertoire," he said. "Doesn't really get the juices flowing, if you know what I mean."

She stiffened. "Forget it. I was just joking," she said, gathering her purse. Not quite sure where she was hoping that conversation thread might lead but absolutely positive she felt like an idiot for bringing it up. "Will you be late tomorrow, as well?" she asked, heading for the door.

"Only Tuesdays and Thursdays."

His wry answer made her turn. "Why only those days?"

He sighed. "Because that's when my dancing partner requires my presence until her regular partner heals from a sprain."

Curiosity got the better of her. "You dance?"

"Only if you use the term loosely," he answered with a shrug. "My mom needed a line dancing partner so I'm filling in until my dad can return."

"You're dancing with your mom?" she asked.

"Yeah."

"Oh." Okay, she had to admit that was kind of sweet. "Are you any good?" she asked.

"About as good as my mom."

"How good is that?"

"My dad has a sprain. Doesn't that tell you something?"

She cracked a smile. "It does," she admitted then opened the door, but before she could leave, she had to know something. He must've sensed she had something on her mind, for he waited to see where she was going. Taking a quick breath, she plunged forward by blurting out, "Why'd you almost kiss me this morning?"

By the look on his face...he was wondering the same thing.

SAMMY MENTALLY SWORE BUT TRIED to keep his expression neutral. Why'd he almost kiss her? Good question. He'd been asking himself that all day but still hadn't come up with an answer so he'd plain given up until the same damn question had popped out of her mouth. "I'm sorry," he said, chewing the inside of his cheek for a minute while he thought of something more intelligent to say. "I got caught up in the moment. It won't happen again," he promised.

He looked up, expecting to see relief on her face but to his eye he could've sworn he read disappointment. Really? He almost did a double take but he didn't. He just waited to see if she'd say something to the effect of *Oh, good. Now I don't need to press charges* or *Wonderful. I would hate to suffer through that again.* Just the thought of her saying any one of those comments made him glum. Thankfully, she said nothing. She merely nodded and let herself out.

AUBREY DROVE HOME, HER MIND full of questions that she didn't want to answer. But in the end, Aubrey couldn't deny what was staring her in the face: she was attracted to Sammy. She groaned, unable to fathom how that had happened. She started out believing he was the worst example of the male species—aside from Derek—that ever walked the planet but slowly her opinion had changed. Apparently she appreciated his rock-hard abs, scruffy chin and tousled hair that was too long to be fashionable and barely looked brushed most of the time. And then there was that killer smile. Yeah, the man could knock a girl down with the wattage coming off those pearly whites and really, that wasn't fair.

And…don't even get her started on his sex appeal. She hated—and when she said *hated,* she really meant it—that he had some kind of sexual charisma women responded to and unfortunately, as much as she'd tried to stay immune, she had somehow succumbed. If it were possible to bottle up what Sammy Halvorsen exuded out of those pores, she'd make millions hawking it to the rest of the world who hadn't won the genetic lottery and had rotten luck with women. Talk about Love Potion No. 9, Sammy Halvorsen–style. Oh, yeah. *Millions*.

She shook her head as if the motion alone might dislodge the alarming direction of her thoughts but Sammy remained. Stubborn man. Her nipples tingled as if he were caressing her through her blouse and she actually gasped at her body's traitorous reaction. She may admit that Sammy was a fine-looking man but she certainly wasn't going to let things go any further. Besides, she thought with a slightly insulted pout, he wasn't interested in going that far with her, either. *Thank goodness for small favors*.

The following morning as Aubrey was preparing to

leave for Sammy's she tried reaching out to her mother, yet again.

In the two weeks since Barbie and Arianna had descended on Emmett's Mill, Barbie had lost much of her sparkle and she seemed to be disintegrating before Aubrey's eyes. Their differences had always made relating to one another difficult but a foreign emotion tugged at Aubrey's heart at the evidence of her mother's heartbreak. "Mother...I'm worried about you," she admitted.

Barbie remained silent and simply pulled her robe tighter around her body. Aubrey hadn't seen her mother out of that robe in days. "Are you sleeping okay?" she asked. She'd recently learned that Barbie had taken to sleeping on the sofa, which couldn't be terribly comfortable for someone who was accustomed to much nicer accommodations. "Do you need anything?" she asked.

Barbie shook her head dispiritedly and Aubrey didn't know what to do. She'd never seen her mother like this. And Arianna was no help. When she wasn't talking on the phone—Aubrey's landline at that because Arianna's cell phone had been shut off for nonpayment—she was complaining about what she didn't have or how abysmal it was to live in Aubrey's house. Frankly, twin or not, Aubrey was ready to toss her sister out on her ear.

"Have you thought of possibly joining a service club or church group?" *Or taking a shower? Eating more than a few slices of apple?* "You're not doing yourself any good acting like this. You need to go clean up, put some makeup on and find something that interests you."

Barbie nodded as if all of those suggestions sounded like good advice but that's where it ended. Aubrey's spirits fell. "Please, Mom?"

At the plea in her voice, Barbie responded and she nodded again, this time with slightly more energy but Aubrey could tell her mom was in a bad way. But who could she turn to for advice? Arianna was useless in this regard. She hated to burden Nora with the situation and she hardly knew Annabelle or Tasha well enough to share such personal information.

Tears welled in her eyes and she turned away quickly before her mother could see them. She'd think of something. She had to.

SAMMY WAS DIRECTING MANNY on the crane when his cell phone buzzed at his hip. He almost ignored it, more concerned about where the guy dropped his load than whoever was trying to get his attention. But then an errant and frightening thought zipped through his mind about Ian and he picked up.

"Yeah?" he said, his eyes never leaving the crane. Manny was still technically learning and accidents cost money. Dean would chew his ass six ways from Sunday if he had to fill out OSHA paperwork. "What?" he repeated, the voice on the other end garbled. "Slow down, I can't understand you. Aubrey? Is everything okay?"

Suddenly, he realized she was crying. He gestured to

Manny to wait for him, then, jogged over to a quieter place and caught the tail end of whatever she had started with.

"You have to come home," she cried. "I have a family emergency. I have to go. Someone needs to be here with the baby. Something's happened to my mom."

"Okay, calm down and take a deep breath. I'll be there in ten minutes."

"Okay," she said with a watery hiccup, then sniffed. "Thank you."

After making arrangements on the job site, he jumped in his truck and headed home.

True to his word, ten minutes later he was walking through the front door. Aubrey, carrying Ian, came around the corner, her eyes wild and red-rimmed with fear. She looked scattered and hardly fit to drive in her current emotional state. "I'll take you," he said, gently lifting Ian from her arms. "You're in no shape to drive. Where am I taking you?"

Aubrey swallowed and opened her mouth, probably to protest but instead she merely jerked her head in a nod. "The hospital. My mother tried to kill herself."

AUBREY WAS TERRIFIED. Was her mother dead? Had she succeeded? Guilt assailed her. She'd known her mother wasn't well but she had no idea her depression had progressed to this level.

Arianna, who had ridden in the ambulance with

their mother, greeted them in the lobby, her expression venomous.

"This is all your fault," she hissed, her eyes wet from tears. "You knew she was depressed and you did nothing about it. She needed her friends around her during this time yet you couldn't loosen your latch on one single penny to fly her home. Are you happy?"

Aubrey stumbled under the force of her sister's anger but even as her lip trembled she spat back, "Don't you go high-and-mighty on me. What friends? She doesn't have any friends back in New York. Has anyone once called to see how she's doing? No. They don't care and being around those blood-sucking, vapid, plastic monsters is the last thing Mother needed!" Ian fussed and drew Aubrey's attention. She choked back the rest of what she wanted to say and forced herself to stick to the details that mattered. "Tell me everything. What happened?"

Arianna threw her a dark look but answered anyway. "Dad's attorney had Mom served today. She opened the envelope and nearly fell over. Then she started screaming. It was awful. And I was locked in that house with her, unable to help, unable to even help myself," she said bitterly.

"Why didn't you call me?" Aubrey asked, frustration with her sister lacing her voice. "I could've been there in fifteen minutes. Maybe I could've helped."

"Help would've been sending us back to New York where we belong," Arianna said, her eyes sparkling with tears. She wiped at the moisture with the flat of her palm. "I think you got pleasure out of seeing us so miserable. Like it was payback or something. Well, congrats, sis. You win. Enjoy your victory."

Aubrey felt the air leave her lungs. Had she subconsciously been punishing them by insisting that they stay here? Grief and shame filled her chest but her eyes remained painfully dry. She couldn't cry. Not here. Not in front of everyone. "I didn't mean to punish either of you," she managed to say, swallowing hard. "It would've been worse if she'd gone back to New York. You came to me for help and that's what I was trying to do."

Arianna didn't bother wiping away the trail of tears sliding down her cheek. Aubrey felt the weight of her sister's accusation. There was no hiding from her twin and the truth was simply ugly. The right words, *I'm sorry,* were stuck in her throat. Disgusted with Aubrey's inability to say anything, Arianna shook her head and finished with the details. "After the major freak-out, she went into the bathroom and swallowed an entire bottle of Valium. When she didn't come out after a half hour, I went to check on her. I found her on the bathroom floor."

Aubrey shuddered. What an awful image to carry around. She tried reaching out to her but Arianna jerked away. "Don't," she warned, though her voice cracked.

Aubrey nodded and walked over to where Sammy stood with Ian in his arms. "She overdosed on Valium," she said in a low voice, not wanting everyone in the waiting room in on their tragic situation, and strangely numb inside. "My dad…he wants a divorce."

Sammy's mouth compressed to a line of sympathy and she wished she could lean on his shoulder for just a minute. She felt so alone. Her sister was spitting pissed at her for keeping them here now that their father had abandoned them, and her mother was so bereft she found death more amenable to living. A ragged sob escaped before she could stop it. "How did everything get so messed up?" she asked mournfully.

Sammy reached over and gently pulled her into an embrace with his free arm, which she went into willingly. "It's going to be okay," he said in a soothing tone. "We have some of the best doctors here in Emmett's Mill in spite of the town's size. She's getting the best of care in there."

"What if she doesn't make it?" she asked fearfully. "What am I going to do? She's my mother. I'm not ready to lose her."

She thought of how she'd always been so distanced from her mother, how they always seemed to be on opposite sides of everything and her heart ached. She should've been more aware that her mother was sliding into a dark place that she couldn't see her way clear from. But she hadn't. She'd been too annoyed with her sister and mother for clinging to a life that was gone. She hadn't been capable of summoning sympathy for either of them when she should've been more compassionate and taken into consideration their need to adjust. She felt like such an evil bitch and that was not a nice feeling.

"I was so cold to her," she whispered. "I was angry

with her. I blamed her for Daddy leaving. Somehow it was all her fault, I just knew it. Maybe Arianna was right and I was punishing her. I could've paid for a plane ticket but...I thought it would be better for them both here. I loved it here so much...I figured...eventually they would, too. God, I'm just as selfish and self-centered as the people I was running away from."

She shuddered and buried her face in his shoulder, his masculine scent a balm to her ragged heart.

"From what I know of you, you aren't selfish," he assured her with a smile in his voice that warmed her inside as he easily disentangled Ian's little fingers from her hair. "You were trying to do what was best. Don't beat yourself up about it. You can't control the actions of others, right? Let's just see how things pan out before we go blaming people. Yourself included."

Aubrey nodded and chuckled softly at Ian's antics, his small baby face such a sweet reprieve from the guilt that was smothering her.

Risking a glance at her sister, who sat alone and tucked into a chair in the corner, she was struck by how terrified and lost Arianna looked. A pang of anguish followed. Arianna wasn't interested in Aubrey's compassion or commiseration. And that hurt, too.

The doctor appeared and walked toward Arianna. Aubrey quickly followed.

"How is our mother?" Aubrey asked. "Is she going to be all right?"

Dr. Hessle, a kindly-looking man with fierce eyebrows, said, "She's resting peacefully now. We had to pump her stomach, which she didn't care for, not that I blame her. Stomach pumping is nasty business for everyone involved. But provided she doesn't try to pull another stunt like this any time soon, she should be fine and ready to go home in the morning. We want to keep her overnight to evaluate her mental state. Technically, we keep a suicidal patient for seventy-two hours but I think she should be fine with her family around. I would recommend that she see a therapist. Sometimes these types of incidents are cries for help."

"The paramedic called my mother 5150. Does that mean she's crazy?" Arianna asked stiffly.

"No, it's a code that's put on all attempted suicides. We have to assume she wasn't thinking clearly when she tried to take her life. That's all that means," he said gently and Arianna nodded reluctantly.

"Can we see her?" Aubrey asked.

"She's resting peacefully right now. How about in the morning? She's in good hands, I assure you."

Aubrey tried not to let her disappointment show but she conceded. The doctor left and Aubrey turned to her sister, who was surreptitiously wiping at her eyes. "You can catch a ride back to the house with us," Aubrey offered.

Arianna shook her head. "I'd rather take a cab."

"We don't have a cab service here, Arianna," Aubrey said. "Don't be stubborn. It's just a car ride. I promise I won't try to talk to you."

Arianna looked trapped and when she finally relented

it was with a stiff set of her shoulders and a pinched expression. "Fine. But not one word."

Aubrey exchanged a look with Sammy and silently thanked him for everything he'd done up until that moment, including being her personal driver.

First thing tomorrow, Aubrey knew they'd have to deal with their mother and it would take both of them to get her through this.

SAMMY DROVE THE ROSE WOMEN home and true to her word, Aubrey didn't try to engage her sister in conversation, but he could sense her sadness coming off her in waves. He was quickly learning that Aubrey had a big heart, one she tried to protect with her aloof nature, but it was there and his son was certainly taking up residence in that privileged space. He had mixed feelings about that. The other day when he'd seen Aubrey press a kiss to Ian's forehead as if it were the most natural thing in the world, his guts had tightened until they were compacted into a ball and he was unable to breathe. It reminded him that his son would never know the woman who had died giving him life. It wasn't fair to either Ian or Aubrey but he hadn't been able to take the pain of that realization and he'd reacted badly, passing a rule that she could no longer kiss his son. Now, he knew what a jackass rule that was. Aubrey was right, kids needed hugs and kisses. Lord knew he'd been smothered with them growing up and he'd loved every minute of it even if he pretended otherwise. What kind of coldhearted bastard was he to deny that basic need from his son?

As soon as Sammy pulled into the driveway, Arianna let herself out to run into the house, slamming the door behind her. Aubrey visibly winced and he felt a twinge of commiseration that was just a bit stronger than it should've been.

"Why's she so hell-bent to blame you for this?" he wanted to know.

Aubrey bit her lip and made a helpless little shrug but she looked miserable. "Our father...well, it came as a shock to all of us that he...decided that he wanted to start a new life—without the entanglements of his former one."

"Are you saying that your dad abandoned you all?" he asked.

"Yeah. I guess I am. I think I'm still numb. My mom thought my dad was going to come to his senses eventually and make everything right again. But when the divorce paperwork came, well, I guess..." She swallowed hard and her voice broke. "I guess she realized he's not coming back."

"That's cold," he murmured, shaking his head. "I can't imagine my dad leaving Ma high and dry much less walking away from his family."

She looked at him with watery eyes. "That's because your dad has ethics and morals and hasn't been corrupted by some woman named Fiona who's probably half his age and tells him that his bald spot is sexy as long as he's buying her things like cars, diamonds and

European spa treatments!" She burst into tears and started bawling into her hands, her shoulders shaking.

Ian, who had fallen asleep during the short drive from town to Aubrey's house, awoke with a startled cry and that made Aubrey cry that much harder. "Now look what I've done," she wailed, reaching back to caress Ian's cheek. She tried crooning to him but her voice was wobbling too much to be comforting and Ian twisted away from her, which only made things worse.

"C'mere," Sammy said, folding her into his arms when she scooted over to him. "It can't be as bad as all that. So your dad is out of the picture. Are you going to miss him? Was he a hands-on kind of father?"

She shook her head. "No. But I always thought he was kind and generous, perhaps too much so when it came to indulging my sister and mother. But now he claims that we're broke and…well, that's why my sister and mother are living with me. I'm the only one they can turn to."

Sammy's mind started clicking, catching on to what she was saying. Aubrey's family was wealthy, er, used to be wealthy? "Do you need money?" he asked, not quite sure how to handle the situation. "I don't have a lot but I can help…."

She waved away his offer with a sniff and pulled away. The look in her eyes was grateful but not one of someone who was desperate. "I have plenty of money to support myself. My father gave Arianna and I an allowance since we were sixteen. Arianna spent hers and always needed more. I was a bit more frugal than that."

Her gaze slid away as if embarrassed. "I have a nice nest egg, if you will. But it wouldn't last a season in New York with my mom and Arianna going through it like water. So...I didn't offer to send them home. Plus, according to my father, all our homes were being sold to pay off the debts. I didn't want to fly them to New York only to find that they had nowhere to go and then have to fly them back. I was just trying to be practical," she said in a pained voice that tugged at his heart.

"Of course you were," he said gruffly. "You did the right thing." He shifted so that she fit into the crook of his shoulder. "So, what about an attorney? Seems that your mom needs one."

"How's she going to pay for it? My father says we're busted."

Sammy doubted that. Not if he was squiring around a new woman on his arm. He had money...somewhere. And he knew just the man who could find it.

"Listen, I want you to go inside and get some rest. Don't worry about Ian. I'll see if Annabelle can help out seeing as you need to go see your mom tomorrow morning. In the meantime, I'm going to make a phone call and someone's going to help you guys out with the lawyer situation. Just so happens my best friend's husband used to be a shark back in the days when he was a hotshot family law attorney in the Bay. If your dad is hiding money...Ben Hollister is the man who can find it."

CHAPTER THIRTEEN

THE NEXT MORNING AUBREY was at the small dining room table sipping her coffee when Arianna wandered in, her hair standing on end and her eyes puffed and swollen. She looked like hell.

Aubrey wanted to talk but she bit her tongue, waiting to see if Arianna would come to her first. She lost hope when Arianna walked past her and went straight to the coffeepot instead. Resigned to another bad day with her sister, she was startled when Arianna sat beside her.

"When are we going to see Mom?" she asked, refusing to look at Aubrey.

"Soon. Visiting hours start at 9:00 a.m. Will you be ready?"

"Yes." And then Arianna left the room to shower.

Aubrey wondered how and when she and her sister had become so different. How could they share the same exact genes yet be polar opposites? A sad smile lifted her mouth as she recalled a time when the differences weren't so marked. It was a happy memory that she treasured because it was so rare now that they were adults. She and Arianna were probably about eight. They had identical dresses and Old Man Jasper, the groundsman, had taken them down to the pond on the property to feed the ducks. It'd been summer and they'd laughed with the sun in their eyes and innocence in their hearts, and they'd giggled with abandon at how the ducks chased after the white chunks of bread as it left their fingertips. Afterward, they'd run hand in hand back to the house for treats that the cook had made earlier for some party their parents were having at the time.

There was no trace of that carefree girl in Arianna any longer, not that she could see. As early as junior high Arianna had started to notice that they were privileged and she reveled in that power over people. Arianna had become a mean girl. And Aubrey had hated it. She still hated it. Maybe forcing her to stay here in Emmett's Mill had been her way of trying to force that aspect of Arianna's personality back underground. She sighed. Either way, whatever her motivation, she'd failed miserably. Her mother was hospitalized and her sister hated her.

She sniffed back the tears before Arianna reappeared, dressed and ready to go.

INSTEAD OF CALLING, SAMMY decided to pay a visit to Nora and Ben in person. He was way overdue for a visit and he'd been a real jerk as of late so he probably deserved whatever might fly out of Nora's mouth. The girl could melt steel with that acidic tongue of hers but he loved her for it just the same. And he respected the hell out of Ben for seeing past that sharp wit and prickly nature to the warmhearted person she was beneath it all.

Pulling up to the old Victorian with its impressive arches and Queen Ann dome, he smiled at how beautiful the house had become under Nora's creative eye. Nora was the best landscape architect in the state of California as far as Sammy was concerned. Her work was heavily sought after, from governors to actors, and she wouldn't ever think of moving from Emmett's Mill. That girl had roots thicker than an oak. Another reason he loved her. They came from similar stock. There was a time—during his misguided, hormone-soaked youth—that he'd fancied himself in love with Nora Simmons. But he'd soon realized that she never saw him like that and he'd come to the bigger realization that they were better as friends than lovers. So instead, they'd grown up as best friends and nothing had changed since.

He knocked and Nora came to the door in overalls with dirt ground into the knee and a long-sleeved white henley.

"Come to apologize for being an ever-loving asshole?" she asked conversationally.

"Of course not," he quipped with a grin.

"Or perhaps you've come to grovel at my feet for a favor," she said, her brow arching.

"Never."

"Ha. Then you've come to mooch a beer off me."

He cocked his gun finger at her. "There, you would be right."

"Excellent. You're in luck, we just had a drop-off."

Sammy walked in, the sound of hundreds of clocks ticking and tocking and some cuckooing filling the room with an oddly soothing cacophony. Still, he teased as he said, "You could go deaf with all this racket. Ever think of having, perhaps, just one clock like normal people?"

Nora stopped and narrowed her gaze at him. "Ever think of having one girlfriend instead of catting around at every honkey-tonk from here to Coldwater, like a normal person?"

"Touché. And for the record, I'm not catting around as you say."

"No? I'll alert the media."

He laughed and accepted the beer she handed him before settling into a nice, fat, overstuffed chair. "So, where's that poor man you managed to wrangle into marrying you?" he asked.

"In the office, counting chickens."

"Chickens?"

Nora sighed. "Yeah. Buster brought a box of chicks as a final payment, said the birds would be worth nearly as much as the eggs when they're grown. Ben didn't have the heart to tell him we're not quite ready to have a bunch of chickens running around the property."

"The coyotes will eat them for sure if you don't get a chicken coop up," he said.

She gestured to her ensemble. "Hence the getup. I was rearranging my beautiful backyard to put in a damn coop. If it weren't for Jackson getting so attached to the little buggers I'd give them to the feed store and let them sell them or something. But—" she sighed, slightly put out "—my son has to have a kind heart and so now we have chickens."

"I never thought I'd say this but you're a good mom, Nora Simmons-Hollister." He tipped his beer toward her in a salute and she cocked a wry grin that he knew spelled trouble.

"Wish I could say the same for you. As far as father-hood goes, you're terrible."

He glowered. "Low blow. Even for you."

"I call 'em as I see 'em but you didn't come here so I could bust your balls. I'll save that for later. But let me warn you, if you don't straighten up, I'm going to remind you who has the better left hook."

"Geesh, what is it about my face that everyone wants to punch it these day? Don't bother. Everyone's been pounding the answer home for you. And, yeah, I deserved it." Sammy huffed a short breath, half-tempted to blow out of there since Nora seemed in a mood to poke at him. They weren't kids anymore and he doubted she had a better left than him...though Nora wasn't above playing dirty. If she were losing in a fight, she wouldn't think twice of just kicking him in the nuts and being done with it. He shuddered at the thought and mentally conceded the victory before the battle had even begun.

"There's help for you yet." Nora grinned. "So what can I do for you?"

"Here's the thing, Aubrey's in need of an attorney," he said.

Nora frowned. "An attorney? Why? Is she in trouble?"

"Not exactly. Apparently, her father ran off and abandoned the family for some other gal and he says they're broke but something tells me he's not as poor as he claims to be."

"Ah, Ben's favorite kind of case," Nora remarked drily.

"Well, the upside is Aubrey won't have to pay you in chickens. She has enough to give Ben a retainer, at least until Ben can dig up some information on her dad."

Nora nodded, and a wide smile followed. "Wow. Cash payment. I've almost forgotten what that's like."

Sammy returned the smile. "Hey, you're the one who convinced that man of yours that country living was the way to go."

"I did no such thing. He made that decision all on his own. Besides, don't let him fool you. He loves it. Although he's not wild about the snow all the time. This morning he and Jackson went to town to find the best snowblower. He doesn't want to shovel the driveway any longer."

"Sounds like a smart purchase. You buy it and then I'll borrow it," he teased.

"Only if you're going to let me borrow that truck of yours to haul fertilizer come spring."

"What happened to Bettina?" Sammy asked, surprised. Bettina was Nora's beat-up old truck that she loved to pieces even though for the past ten years it had been *falling* to pieces.

Nora made an unhappy face. "She finally died. And I think Ben was just a little too happy to give her to scrap if you ask me. Now he wants to go look at new trucks but my heart's just not in it yet. I'm grieving for crying out loud."

"You poor thing," Sammy said drily. "I feel your pain. Who'd want a brand-new truck with windows that don't require a wrench or pliers to operate or a bench seat that doesn't have springs poking your ass every time you move? That's just nuts. Maybe you can go by the junkyard and find one of Bettina's busted-up relatives to haul your stinky poop load around."

Nora laughed easily. "Yeah, life's rough."

They finished their beers and then Sammy got up to leave. "You think Ben can take on the case?" he asked in all seriousness.

She regarded him with that keen gaze that never failed to see through any level of bullshit and then nodded. "For Aubrey, yes. She's a good person. I like her," she said, as if giving her a stamp of approval.

"She's a good nanny. I'd hate to lose her over this whole family mess of hers," he returned neutrally, seeing from a mile away where this was going.

Nora leaned against the door frame as Sammy let himself out. "You know, she's good with Ian. A natural."

"Yeah, I think all nannies should like being around kids, don't you think?"

"It's more than that. I think her heart is invested in your son."

"Yeah. I get that sense, too. Maybe a little too much. What should I do about it?"

Nora made a sound of annoyance at his question, then raised her shoulder in a flip shrug. "Don't screw it up. I'll have Ben give her a call when he gets back."

And then she closed the door, leaving Sammy to wonder if there'd been some hidden meaning behind Nora's words. Usually, Nora was pretty blunt, but lately she'd been trying tact on for size and the result was a lot of cryptic comments or answers. Frankly, he missed the old Nora. At least he knew what the hell she was saying.

He climbed into his truck and drove toward Josh's house to pick up Ian, Nora's words echoing in his head.

AUBREY AND HER SISTER WALKED into Barbie's room and both gasped at the haggard figure lying in the bed. Arianna's hand went to her mouth and Aubrey bit her lip to keep from crying. She tried keeping Sammy's words of advice close to her heart but guilt was dragging on her heels.

Arianna moved to Barbie's side, forcing Aubrey to take the other side, near the window.

"Mom?" Arianna whispered, running a knuckle down her face softly to wake her up. "It's Arianna."

"And Aubrey," Aubrey added quickly, scowling at her sister but it was lost on her. Barbie's eyes fluttered open and Aubrey read despair, embarrassment…shame. "How are you feeling?" she asked.

"How do you think she's feeling?" Arianna cut in

before Barbie could answer. "She's feeling pretty rotten I imagine. How chipper would you feel if you'd just spent the night in the hospital in a strange town without anyone you know at your side?"

Aubrey compressed her lips in fury at her sister but kept silent for her mother's sake. She could tell Barbie didn't have the strength to referee her grown daughters and Aubrey wasn't about to put her in a position to have to do so.

"Arianna, could you find me something to drink? My throat hurts," Barbie said, her voice hoarse. Arianna nodded and left to find water.

Barbie grasped Aubrey's hand, the contact startling Aubrey. She couldn't remember the last time her mother reached out to touch her in any way much less with affection. "I'm so sorry," she whispered, tears squeezing from her eyes. "I lost my mind. I didn't know where to turn or what to do."

"It's okay, Mom," Aubrey said, patting her mother's hand, fighting her own tears. "I understand."

Barbie shook her head. "No, it's not okay. It's not. And I want you to know that I know that."

Aubrey's throat constricted and all she could do was nod. "I'm just glad you made it. I'm not ready to be without a mother," she managed to squeak out. Barbie's weak smile undid her, though. The tears flowed unchecked. "Mom...I'm so sorry I didn't realize how much you were struggling.... I—"

"Shh." Barbie squeezed her hand gently. "You're my

child, no matter how old you are. It's not your job to watch over me. It was my choice and it was a bad one. I'm ashamed for trying to take the easy way out."

Aubrey nodded and Arianna returned with a cup of water and some ice.

"Thank you, Arianna," Barbie said, accepting the cup and taking a dainty sip, wincing as she swallowed. "My throat is still a little tender," she explained. "Apparently, they stuck some thing down my throat and it was quite painful. The doctor said it could be a few days before my throat heals completely."

"Jell-O diet for you coming up," Aubrey said, trying to joke, but her heart was still weeping inside. She drew a deep breath and wiped at her eyes. "If you want, I'll pay for your plane ticket back to New York." She glanced at her sister. "I'll pay for both of you if you want to go."

Arianna made a sound of relief. "Hallelujah. It's about time you came to your senses. Mom, don't worry about a thing. I'll take care of the arrangements," she said, moving as if to find a computer terminal, she was so anxious to get the hell out of Emmett's Mill, but Barbie stopped her with a soft word.

"Wait."

Arianna paused at the door, her brow furrowing in confusion. Barbie shook her head. "I'm not going back to New York. There's nothing there for me any longer."

"That's not true, you have your friends, your committees, your clubs," Arianna protested, a look of panic starting to cross her features. "Mom...our *life* is back in New York. Not here."

"Not anymore. Not for me. If your sister wants to pay for your trip back, that's her business but I'm not going back to a place where I have no one and nothing to call my own. Not one of my friends has called, not one has cared enough to see if I was alive or dead because to them, I am defunct. The houses are gone. It was all in the paperwork that your father's lawyer sent over. I can't hold lavish parties, can't donate to ridiculous causes, and everyone by now knows what your father has done to us. The shame of it is too much to bear. I won't go and subject myself to their scrutiny."

"So you'd rather down a whole bottle of Valium and die in the middle of nowhere!" Arianna nearly shouted, eliciting a sharp look from Aubrey, but she didn't seem to care. "I can't stay here! I have friends! I have a life! I have...people who care!" Her voice took on a shrill note then she stopped abruptly and narrowed her wild gaze at Aubrey. "If your offer still stands, I want a ticket out of here *tonight.*"

Arianna collected what dignity she had left and stalked from the room with a terse "I'll be waiting in the car." And then she was gone.

Aubrey looked to her mom. "I'm sorry. She's been in quite a mood lately. I think she's flipped her crackers, to be honest."

Barbie's mouth lifted in a sad smile. "She'll get to New York and realize the same thing I did while sitting in that bathroom, contemplating my life and the ruin of it. I know you've been more frugal with your allowance than either me or Arianna…. Would you be willing to pay for a round-trip ticket for your sister so that she has a place to come to when she makes that realization?"

"Of course, Mom," Aubrey said, seeing her mother with new eyes. "But I don't think Arianna will come to that realization as quickly as you did. She's got more pride than anyone I know. She'll live on the streets before admitting that she was wrong."

At that Barbie shook her head. "She's stubborn but she'll never sleep in the streets. Your sister will come back before it comes to that. Don't worry. She'll come around."

Aubrey didn't have her mother's faith, but truth be told, she was ready for a break from Arianna. Her sister was seriously getting on her nerves and a cool-off for them both would do them good.

"Mom, a friend of mine's husband is a lawyer. I want you to talk to him," she said.

"Honey, I don't have the money for that. Besides, what's to quibble over? Harold says we're broke and the money is gone. It's all laid out quite plainly in the paperwork I read. No sense in throwing good money after bad." She sighed with remorse. "I just wish I'd known we were in such dire straits. Your father never said a thing. He always encouraged me to maintain appearances and to do that you have to keep to a certain standard."

Aubrey bit her lip, remembering how lavishly they'd lived. She'd always assumed it was her mother who'd insisted on all these things because her father had so often complained to her of that fact but now she wasn't so sure. How untruthful had her father been to them all? She blinked back tears, more determined than ever to see her mom through this.

"Listen, I want to do this. I've already made arrangements to pay the retainer. And…I don't think Dad is being entirely truthful about your finances. This guy, Ben Hollister, used to be a shark in San Francisco, and he's good at finding what people don't want others to find…like money for soon-to-be ex-wives."

Barbie winced and her eyes watered, which made Aubrey want to sock her father for being such an insensitive lout. "Please, Mom, what will it hurt to poke around?" she asked.

Barbie wiped at her eyes. "All right," she conceded. "But I'm not getting my hopes up. That life is over."

"I know, Mom," Aubrey murmured, leaning down to kiss her mother's forehead. "But what Dad did…it's just not right. I love him but I want to kill him for doing this to you."

Barbie's eyes shone with warmth. "You're a good daughter. I'm sorry it took me so long to recognize it."

"Better late than never," she teased, smiling.

She had a mother. And she was going to help her fight.

CHAPTER FOURTEEN

THANKSGIVING WAS FAST approaching and Sammy felt the weight of it, more tangible than an iron cowbell clanging around his neck. It had been Dana's favorite holiday, not because she had so many warm memories of childhood Thanksgivings—actually, quite the opposite—but she'd always told him that Thanksgiving was the kind of holiday that represented everything she'd ever wanted and never had: a large family centered around an expansive table that nearly groaned under the weight of all the home-cooked food, a giant turkey basted in its own juices until it turned golden brown, stuffing and pumpkin pie, laughter and games, family stories told while the older relatives snoozed in armchairs after all the food was eaten. Basically, everything Sammy had grown up having and taking for granted. Those few short years with Dana had shown him how precious those connections were but now that she was gone…he didn't know if he could bear spending the holiday without her.

His thoughts moved to Aubrey and everything she'd been through in the past few weeks, most of which he'd never even known was going on because she wasn't the type to air her dirty laundry, and contemplated inviting her to Thanksgiving dinner at his parents' house. He'd been thinking of some way to get out of it but it shamed him to think of how Dana would feel if she knew her son was missing out on his first holiday. That was one thing she was adamant about. She'd wanted their children to grow up feeling loved and cherished, with plenty of good memories from their childhood. So far, he was doing a bang-up job, as Nora would say. He scrubbed his hands across his face, still not quite sure what to do.

He didn't have long to remain morose. Aubrey walked in, her expression the usual mask of professionalism that he was beginning to realize was her way of protecting herself and it made him wish she'd just smile. When she wasn't so pensive, she had a beautiful smile. He'd have never guessed, to be honest, that the woman even had teeth from when he first met her. She wasn't anything resembling flirty—Dana hadn't been, either— and he'd found that intriguing. He pulled up short as he started to make more comparisons in his head. *She's not Dana. She's nothing like Dana.* And that was a damn good thing, he wanted to growl. It's not like he could replace the love of his life with someone who merely shared similar characteristics.

"How's your mom?" he asked, showing polite interest. And it was simply being polite. "She doing okay since you brought her home?"

She smiled briefly, that small movement more of a ghost of a smile than anything else, and he sensed that she knew he was just being considerate. "She's doing better. Thank you. But if there's any way you could come straight home, I would appreciate it. I don't like to leave her alone for too long."

"Of course. Actually, if it starts raining, I'll be home earlier than usual. Can't work construction in the rain."

"Oh. Right. That would be great."

He turned to leave but as he passed Ian, he paused and his son looked up at him from his swing. Big, wide eyes watched him inquisitively. He ruffled the boy's fine hair and then left.

FOR A LONG MOMENT AFTER Sammy left, Aubrey suffered from a disquieting sense that she yearned for more from him. Something more than a perfunctory *have a nice day*. But then, why would she yearn for something that was never offered, and even if he had offered, she wouldn't accept? Such thinking was the kind of stuff that usually got her into trouble, so she pushed it away and gave her undivided attention to Ian, who happily and without reservation went into her arms for a quick cuddle before breakfast.

It was later that afternoon while Ian was taking a nap and Aubrey was working on the blanket she was knitting that she had an unexpected visitor.

She went to the door and found Sammy's mother, Mary, stamping the mud from her boots on the porch, her cheeks rosy from the cold. Aubrey ushered Mary in and they went to the living room.

"What brings you by?" she asked, putting on the kettle for some hot tea. "You should've called. I'd have put in some apple scones."

"Bless you but I don't need any apple scones these days." Mary laughed, patting at her ample hips. "Besides, Thanksgiving is just around the corner and there's no getting around the fact that I put two sticks of butter in the mashed potatoes."

Aubrey's mouth watered at the thought of that holiday spread. Her own holidays had been dress-up affairs that were stuffy and mostly all about appearances. Sure, they looked the part but at a very young age Aubrey realized there was no substance to them. She started opting out, slinking away when she couldn't flat-out refuse. She'd watch from the balcony of their expansive apartment as people in designer clothes who'd arrived by limousine laughed, drank and mixed business with pleasure in some semblance of an intimate dinner, but the laughter was fake and while the food was delicious, the company was lacking.

"I'm not complaining but I'm curious what brings you by. Ian is asleep but I could see if I could rouse him for a visit with his grandmother if you like," she said, moving to wake him, but Mary waved her offer away.

"Rule number one—never wake a sleeping baby," she admonished playfully. "That's something I take to heart. No, actually, I'm here to invite you and your family to Thanksgiving dinner at our house this year. I heard about your mother's unfortunate incident and I figured now was not the time to be alone. She needs to be surrounded by people, not sitting home alone, staring out the window."

At first her heart gladdened at the invitation then she realized Sammy might not appreciate such an offer. If he didn't want her getting too attached to Ian how would he react if he thought she was horning in on his family? "That's so generous of you, but we couldn't," she murmured, with a private sigh. "It just wouldn't feel right to intrude on Sammy's family like that."

"Sammy doesn't control who I invite to my home," Mary said with a smile. "Don't worry about Sammy. He'll come around. He always does."

At that cryptic comment Aubrey almost pressed for a little clarification but then she figured she didn't want to know.

"That's such a lovely offer. I don't know what to say," she said.

"Nonsense. Just say yes and it'll be settled." Mary smiled as if the matter was agreed upon, then moved on to a different topic. This time the smile left her voice. "Is there anything I can do for your mom? Have you invited her to come out to the Quilters Brigade? Busy hands settle an uneasy mind, you know."

"I've tried. She's not quite the quilting type. You have to understand, my mom comes from a life composed of New York's elite. She wouldn't even know how to fit in, much less quilt or knit. She'd stick out like a sore thumb and I think that will just make her feel more alienated but I appreciate the offer."

Mary patted Aubrey's knee affectionately. "Honey, I don't mean to be rude but there's more to the Quilters Brigade than first meets the eye. Sure, we're a bunch of community members who do charitable things and organize committees and whatnot but you'd be surprised what's hiding in some of our closets."

"How do you mean?" Aubrey asked, confused. Her idea of a quaint quilting circle fading in light of this new information. A part of her didn't want to know what secrets lurked within that seemingly innocuous group. She didn't want to lose the stereotype she was quietly fostering—and enjoying.

"Oh, don't look so stricken, dear. There are no murderers in our group but women are a complicated lot. You can never take what you see at face value as gospel. I'm not one to traffic in gossip but I will tell you this, your mother is not alone in her struggles. You'd be surprised to hear that one or two of our circle has, at one time, tried to ride off into the sunset with Prince Valium."

Aubrey tried not to stare. She mentally checked off the names and faces of the people she knew, trying to ascertain who might've been the one to attempt suicide, but came up empty.

Mary smiled knowingly. "Don't waste your energy trying to figure it out. We at the Quilters Brigade are bound to silence to protect our own. So, please tell your mother she's welcome anytime. We're always open to having another strong, intelligent woman join our fold."

Aubrey felt tears sting her eyes at Mary's kindness. "Thank you," she whispered. "I will let her know."

"Great. In the meantime, please do us the pleasure of your company at Thanksgiving dinner. We would love to have you."

"If we decide to come...should I bring anything?"

"Just your appetite." Mary grinned impishly, then added, "On second thought, a nice bottle of wine would be wonderful."

"You got it."

Aubrey saw Mary to the door and waved as the older woman drove away. She stood at the window for a long time, watching the clouds roll in with the promise of a storm in their dark gray folds, and sighed when she considered all that had happened since coming to Emmett's Mill.

She came here to escape her life—or the mess she'd made of it—and found what she'd always been looking for. The only problem, it belonged to someone else.

Not for the first time since meeting the Halvorsens, Aubrey found herself envying a dead woman. It was shameful and what she believed was beneath her but when she looked at the pictures, listened to the stories and got to know Sammy and his family better, she desperately wanted to insert herself into that life. How pathetic.

She heard Ian whimpering and went to his bedroom to get him. Snuggling him tight, she kissed away his sleepy tears and wondered what had given him bad dreams. He coughed and she detected a subtle phlegm quality to it. She frowned, making a mental note to tell Sammy about it.

CHAPTER FIFTEEN

SAMMY WALKED INTO HIS HOUSE a bundle of nerves with a headful of chatter pushing him one way and then the other. His mother had invited Aubrey to Thanksgiving dinner, a little tidbit he'd been given over a quick phone call at lunch, and one that he had not appreciated. Well, he appreciated the warning, but he would've preferred if his mother had kept the guest list *family only*.

Didn't she understand how difficult this was going to be for him? He pushed open the door and stalked inside, ignoring Aubrey's pleasant hello as he sequestered himself inside his bedroom. Covered in grime, he showered quickly, hoping the water would wash away the dirt and the feelings weighing him down, but as he toweled off, he realized he was still fighting the same morose attitude. He understood his mother's motives. Aubrey and her mother had recently been through a harrowing personal ordeal, but having Aubrey around in the context of something social made Sammy jumpy. How was he supposed to keep the lines firmly drawn between them if he was forced to notice how when the light caught her hair just right it was like watching golden rain fall in pools of sunlight? He shook his head in irritation. Now look at him, he was a friggin' poet. No. He was her employer; she was his nanny. End of story. And he could keep the lines drawn. It was imperative to his sanity.

AUBREY BIT HER LIP IN consternation at the slam of the bedroom door as Sammy disappeared with barely a terse hello. Somehow she knew what was biting him and it made her frown unhappily. She'd known Mary's invitation was going to upset him. She also knew this was Sammy's first Thanksgiving without his wife and it was probably pretty difficult to handle, so she didn't begrudge him his surly manner. But she had to admit, it stung a little to know that he didn't want her around at a family function.

Like a pathetic fool she'd been dreaming about sampling those lips, imagining what it would feel like to be pressed against that hard body and firm mouth. That ridiculous little tease he'd given her a month and a half ago was simply inadequate for her needs.

She stretched and yawned before going to pick up Ian, who had tired of his usual playthings and had started to fuss. She cuddled with him on the sofa and decided to read him a book while she waited for Sammy to get out of the shower. As she opened the child's picture book, filled with images of barnyard animals that talked, she tried to keep her mind focused on the story rather than the knowledge that Sammy was in his shower…naked. Her cheeks flushed and she bent her head to start the story.

AUBREY CAME HOME TO FIND Ben and Nora Hollister talking with her mother, the look on Barbie's face caught somewhere between hopeful and crushed.

"Hey, guys, what's going on?" she asked, setting her purse on the table before entering the living room. "Mom? Everything okay?"

Barbie smiled tremulously and gestured to the Hollisters. "Mr. Hollister thinks he may have found where your father is hiding money. And if he's correct, you were right. We aren't as broke as he wanted me to believe."

Tears filled her mother's eyes and Aubrey sat by her side. "That's a good thing, right?" she asked gently.

Her mother nodded. "Yes, of course it is, sweetheart. But I can't help but feel...even more betrayed. How could he do this to me after all our years together? I had his children. I kept his home. I did everything he ever asked of me and more. I don't understand how it all came down to this."

Ben and Nora exchanged looks of commiseration and Aubrey felt her own eyes filling with tears. "I don't know, Mom. I'm still trying to understand his motives, too. All I can figure is that he's not the man we all thought he was."

Ben spoke up. "I've seen many men do exactly this sort of thing to their wives. It's altogether too common. But I used to do this for a living before Nora forced a conscience on me." He grunted as Nora punched him in the bicep with a glower. "Ouch. Just kidding, sweetheart. The day I found you was the best day of my life."

Nora groaned. "Laying it on a little thick don't you think? C'mon, Aubrey's not paying you for your acting skills. Tell her the best news."

Ben smiled. "You see, your father wasn't half as skilled as some of my former clients' husbands. I don't know the amount yet but I've found the account he's using to squirrel away funds. I should be able to procure the amount in a few days."

"Thank you so much," Aubrey said, relieved for her mother's sake. She'd already decided to section out some of her own nest egg to put into an account in her mother's name to get her back on her feet but this was even better. "We appreciate everything you've done. This means a lot to the both of us."

Barbie, although smiling at first, seemed troubled. "Will we have to go to court?" she asked.

"Likely not," Ben said. "I have a feeling your ex isn't going to want to go to court over this. He wants a low profile so once I apply a little pressure in the right spots, he'll cave."

Nora kissed him on the cheek, her eyes glowing. "I love it when you talk all lawyerly."

Barbie's smile returned, even if it didn't quite sparkle with victory. "You're sure?"

"I know his type," Ben assured her. "He's banking on the fact that you'd probably never have thought to doubt his word, especially when he was the one who was always in charge of the finances, am I right?"

Barbie looked chagrined. "Yes...he gave me an

allowance. I never had cause to look into our finances. He was the one who handled all those things."

"Don't worry. It's going to work out just fine. I've got a gut feeling on this one." Ben took Barbie's hand and patted it gently. "We're not going to let him get away with this."

Barbie ducked her head, sniffing back tears. "Thank you," she managed to whisper. Nora discreetly gestured to Ben that it was time to go and Aubrey appreciated her sensitivity. Barbie excused herself to the bathroom and Aubrey walked the Hollisters to the door. Ben went to the car while Nora stayed back for a moment.

Tucking her hands into the back pockets of her jeans, Aubrey sighed heavily. "I can't tell you how much it means..."

"We know," Nora interjected softly, her gaze sincere. "Here's the thing, I know you love your dad. It's hard to still love someone you're so angry with. I was angry with my dad for years for something that happened when my oldest sister was in college. At some point, you'll be ready to forgive and move on, even if he's not an active player in your life."

"Thanks, Nora." Aubrey stared down at her shoes, mulling over the advice. She looked up. "You're becoming one of my favorite people in Emmett's Mill."

Nora gave a cheeky grin. "I know. I'm hard to resist."

Aubrey laughed at that and playfully pushed her out the door.

Barbie emerged from the bathroom, face freshly scrubbed but her eyes were still red.

"Mom, do you want to talk?" she asked hesitantly.

Barbie took to the couch, settling in with a wistful expression. "You know, all those years I tried to live up to your father's expectations that I lost sight of who I was. In the beginning I never wanted the parties or the connections. I just wanted to be able to buy a nice home for our children and provide a stable life. Somewhere along the way, I think we both lost sight of who we were."

Aubrey was still coming to grips that she never truly knew her mother, or her father for that matter, but she'd judged them both unfairly. "I never knew that wasn't your idea. Dad always made it sound as if it was all your idea."

Barbie shook her head. "No. Not that I'm blameless for what we did years later. I became accustomed to the life. I had to or else I'd have shamed your father right out of those expensive business deals that kept us in the lap of luxury. But to be honest, there were so many times I was ready to walk away from it all. But I just couldn't do that to you and Arianna. Especially Arianna."

"Mom, I would've rather lived simply and gotten to know the real you than watched the fake you from afar. I missed having a mother," she said truthfully.

Barbie was silent for a long moment. "All I can say is I wish I could change the way it all turned out but what is done is done."

Aubrey nodded. "You're right, Mom. Have you heard

from Arianna?" she asked, worry for her sister overriding her extreme annoyance with her actions and accompanying attitude. Barbie shook her head and Aubrey sighed. "Well, I hope she finds what she's looking for back in New York. I guess it wasn't in the cards for her to find it here."

Barbie looked at her speculatively. "Have *you* found what you were looking for?"

"What do you mean?"

"Honey, I may not have been the most attentive mother as of late but I did notice that you left town right after you broke up with Derek."

Aubrey shrugged, hating that part of her own personal history. Derek was still a sore spot, the wretched heartbreaker. "I wasn't looking for anything except a place that was radically different from Manhattan," she murmured.

Barbie didn't appear satisfied with her answer but didn't press. Instead, she said, "Sometimes even if we don't know we're looking for something, it lands in our lap just the same."

Aubrey chuckled at that. "And sometimes it passes us right on by," she said with a soft sigh. Sounded a lot like her own personal theme song. Impulsively, she hugged her mother. "Don't worry, Mom. Everything I need is right here with you. I'm happy."

Sort of.

IT WAS LATE AND SAMMY was awake. Ian had long since crashed. He appreciated the fact that Aubrey always gave him a bath just before he arrived so that the little kid would be tuckered out and ready to hit the sack soon after. He supposed he was lucky. The kid didn't wake up once he was asleep. In that way Ian was just like him. A freight train could truck on by but if he was snoozing, he wouldn't notice a thing.

He wandered the house aimlessly with no outlet for the turmoil of his thoughts. Thanksgiving was tomorrow. He wished he could just skip over the whole thing. Forget that it was ever on the calendar.

He remembered last year's Thanksgiving, so different from the one he was facing. Dana had been seven months pregnant and glowing, the joy evident in the smile she beamed his way, the laughter reflecting from her gaze. He'd been so drunk on her love that he'd pushed away the fear caused by her delicate pregnancy. She didn't want him to be focused on what could go wrong; she'd wanted to enjoy every moment of her pregnancy because she'd waited so long to have a child and there was nothing that she would gripe about. She didn't make a peep when she had morning sickness throughout her second trimester; she didn't complain when her sciatic nerve started to spasm, causing sharp stabbing pains to puncture her lower back; she didn't want to focus on anything negative.

And he'd been willing to indulge her because he was just happy to see her happy. He hadn't given much thought to the warning that the doctors had given them about type 1 diabetes and pregnancy. Dana had always waved away his concerns, saying it was something she'd lived with for so long she almost forgot she had it. Except for when she had to stick a needle in her thigh, she'd joked, but Sammy's accompanying laughter had always been a little uneasy. He'd trusted her to know what she could handle.

He'd had no idea that Thanksgiving would be their last. His eyes teared up and he sniffed back the moisture gathering at the corners. Would he ever stop missing her? It seemed impossible.

And now there was Aubrey. Who was so different from the women he kept in his life for selfish reasons. A part of him hated himself for drowning his grief in women and liquor. Certainly it wasn't something he could be proud of. Since Aubrey had come around, he'd stopped going to the bar, having lost interest in the chase of nameless conquests, but that left him at home…to think.

And that sucked.

Thinking made him remember and remembering caused him to hurt.

He knew there was a reason he avoided those things.

If only he could go back to the way he was before Aubrey. But that was impossible, too.

Shit. Tomorrow he'd have to face that turkey holiday and there was no way of getting around it. Not if he wanted to ever hold his head up around his family again. He sighed. Well, hopefully it was like ripping a Band-Aid off—do it fast and it'll only hurt for a second. Pull it slow and it'll take hair and skin with it.

CHAPTER SIXTEEN

IT TOOK SOME DOING BUT SOMEHOW she managed to talk her mom into accompanying her to the Halvorsens' for Thanksgiving, though it broke her heart to see Barbie so unsure of herself in a social setting. She was accustomed to her mother being the gracious hostess, not the uncomfortable guest.

"We don't have to stay long," Aubrey offered, touching her mother's sleeve gently. "Just say the word and I'll make our excuses."

Barbie smiled uncertainly but put on a brave face. "It was kind of your friends to invite us," she said. "I'll be fine."

Mary Halvorsen appeared at the door and ushered them inside the warm and inviting interior of the Halvorsen family home. Aubrey couldn't help but feel a twinge of curiosity to explore the pictures lining the walls to see if she could pick out some vintage Sammy, preferably ones where he was a scrawny kid with braces or something like that.

"I'm so glad you could make it," Mary said, beaming when she noted the vintage French pinot noir in Barbie's hands. "Ah, you brought the wine. Excellent. Let me show you to the kitchen." And with that Mary took control of Barbie, much to Aubrey's surprise, and she was sent into the living room where everyone else was watching football on the giant-screen television.

The Halvorsen crew—father, brothers and assorted young adult offspring—were a beer commercial in the making. They were all wearing football jerseys of various teams yelling at plays on the field, chomping on pretzels in between disagreements while little Jasmine played on the floor with Ian. Aubrey's first instinct was to go and pick up Ian but she hung back, unsure of her role in this setting, but Sammy gestured for her to join them.

"Pick your side," he advised her as she took a seat opposite him. "This is Patriots territory but we tolerate others as long as you're not a Raiders fan," he teased, which elicited a groan from Josh.

"Don't go picking on my Raiders now. They're going to have a comeback, just wait and see," Josh said, defending his team.

Aubrey smiled. "I don't actually have a team favorite," she admitted, but refrained from mentioning that she'd never actually acquired a taste for the game. Watching the Halvorsen family, including the father, become so animated about the game, she warmed from the inside out. This was what hometown America was about, she thought giddily and wondered how she might've turned out differently if this had been her home life instead of what she'd experienced. Her gaze collided with Sammy's, and she blushed when she discovered he was watching her with an intensity that made her wonder if she'd done something wrong or if he wanted to tear her clothes off. Truthfully, she wasn't sure which she preferred. A shiver gently rocked her body and she braved a small smile as she went and plucked Ian from the floor, regardless of how it may look. She was fairly addicted to Ian's slobbery kisses and her day wasn't complete until she'd gotten one. Preferring to have him in her arms, she found her way to the kitchen where Annabelle and Tasha were helping Mary prepare one monster of a feast. Aubrey's eyes bugged at the huge bowl Mary was manhandling in order to mash the potatoes. Mary grinned at Aubrey's expression, saying, "My boys like their mashed potatoes. Always got to make sure there's enough for at least a few helpings apiece."

Aubrey exchanged a look with Barbie, who although still reserved in her manner, had taken on the job of preparing the fruit salad. For a second Aubrey had to force herself not to stare. She'd never seen her mother in a kitchen where she actually did the cooking. She didn't know her mother *could* cook. But there she was chopping fruit like a celebrity chef with an efficiency that astounded Aubrey.

"Stop staring at your ma like that," Mary teased as she whipped and mashed those spuds with a vengeance. "You act as if you've never seen her in a kitchen before."

Aubrey laughed ruefully. If only Mary knew what kind of lifestyle they'd led… "It's been a while," was all Aubrey said and Barbie chuckled softly. "So, is there anything I can do to help?"

Mary shook her head. "I think we have it under control. In fact, why don't you girls leave the rest for us old ladies. We've got it under control, don't we, Barbie?"

Barbie nodded and started adding the bananas. "I think so."

Aubrey looked to her mother. "Are you sure? I could stay and help. I don't mind," she said, purely for her mother's sake. She wasn't sure if she was emotionally strong enough to deal with the whirlwind that was Mary Halvorsen, but Barbie simply waved her away. Tasha and Annabelle pushed Aubrey out of the kitchen.

Tasha murmured out of the side of her mouth, "That's our cue to get the heck out of her kitchen. She only lets us do so much then it's out you go. But she's a phenomenal cook so I leave her to it."

Annabelle giggled. "Amen to that. I'm a wreck in the kitchen and Mary only trusts me with the most simple of jobs like opening cans of green beans and pouring them into a bowl."

Aubrey laughed, feeling more at home with these people than she ever did with anyone in New York.

SAMMY TRIED TO KEEP HIS attention focused on the game—and he did a fair enough job of appearing as if he were engrossed—but his true focus was Aubrey. He must've been blind the first day they met because if she'd looked half this good he'd have thought twice before hiring her. And it kinda made him angry at her for being so beautiful. Why'd she have to go and dress like that? Like she didn't know that that black sweater made her skin look like alabaster or that the way her jeans caressed her petite body was nearly a sin in every way imaginable—at least what he wanted to do to her was certainly sinful—or that when she smiled it radiated to her gaze and made him cramp with need.

Josh roared at the television and punched Sammy in the arm, startling him enough to make him yelp, which only made Josh roll with laughter. "Poor baby brother, did I get you too hard?" he teased, then gestured to the television. "I told you the wide receiver wasn't worth what they're paying him. I've seen better legs on a chair. Someone needs to light a fire under his pads to get him moving."

"Yeah, whatever. Stick to your Raider Nation and go paint your face." He rose to get another beer, studiously avoiding looking at Aubrey for fear of scowling or drooling, both of which would earn him no small amount of crap from his brothers. "You need a fresh one, Dad?" he asked but his father declined.

"I'll take one," Josh said with a grin.

"Last I checked your legs weren't broken," Sammy returned with a half smirk.

Josh shrugged. "Fine. Be that way but don't come my way when you're needing to use my backhoe for those side landscaping jobs you like to rack up with Nora Hollister. Come to think of it…I don't think I've ever seen a dime—"

"One beer coming up," Sammy interjected with good humor and walked into the kitchen.

Before going to the fridge, he peered over his ma's shoulder for a whiff of those whipped potatoes. They smelled so good, he risked losing a limb and swiped a finger along the bowl for a good dollop and stuck it in his mouth.

"Samuel Halvorsen, you get your finger out of there before I cut it off," Mary scolded, batting at him with an oven mitt. "Go on, shoo!"

Sammy winked and reached into the fridge for two beers. "I couldn't resist. Your mashed potatoes are the best."

Mary warmed visibly and smiled. "Charmer," she said, her tone saying perhaps that was a liability instead of a virtue. "Now get out."

Sammy ducked out and after handing his brother the fresh beer, he found himself wandering over to check out what the women, including Aubrey, were crowded around in the corner. He groaned when he saw that it was a photo album.

The look of amusement on Aubrey's face did not bode well for him. He was fairly certain she'd stumbled across the picture of him when he was seven and he'd gotten into his mother's eye makeup. He looked like a pint-size clown with no sense of style. He peered over her shoulder and tried not to inhale the lightly sweet scent that emanated from her body and then sighed when he saw that he was right.

"Hey, my brothers had a hand in that," he declared when she dissolved into a fit of giggles. "I'm pretty sure they probably held me down and did that to me."

Dean twisted to look at Aubrey and grinned. "The makeup picture. That was the best. We tried to get him into a dress, too, but we couldn't find one that would fit."

Annabelle draped her arms around her husband's neck as she stood over him on the back side of the sofa and gave him a resounding smack of a kiss before straightening and ruffling his hair. "I bet you made your mama proud," she said wryly.

"Damn straight," Dean said. "You should've seen when we held Josh down and sheared off his eyebrows. He looked like a garden gnome when we were through with him."

Josh scowled even as Tasha laughed, remembering. "God, I'd forgotten about that! Oh, Josh, you did look pretty funny, sweetheart. It's a good thing you were a cute kid even without eyebrows. Your future status as prom king might have been in jeopardy."

Josh reached out and grabbed Tasha, pulling her squealing into his lap, one hand firmly on her tush and his mouth sealing hers for a hot kiss that only made Sammy ache for his loss. Glancing away, he realized Aubrey witnessed his yearning and it embarrassed him to be caught with his feelings so clearly written on his face.

His cheeks flared and he excused himself before he said or did something he'd regret.

AUBREY SAW SAMMY HEAD OUTSIDE and, resisting the good advice in her head telling her to mind her own business, she did the exact opposite and followed.

She found him sitting on the fender of an old Ford in the backyard, tossing small rocks into the field beyond the house. Aubrey gingerly took a seat beside him and held her hand out. He placed a few pebbles into her hand.

"Everything okay?" she asked after she'd tossed one into the field. "You kind of disappeared."

He shrugged and threw a rock, waiting until it skittered into the field with a soft clack before answering. "My head's still not right. This is the first Thanksgiving since Dana died and it hits me at weird times."

She rolled the smooth gray rock between her fingers. "No one expects you to forget her and move on so quickly," Aubrey said. "You have to give yourself time to grieve."

Sammy quirked a sad smile. "Yeah, so they say."

"I imagine it's not easy," she murmured.

"It's like trying to forget that you've lost a limb, or it feels as if someone reached into your chest and ripped out your heart without anesthesia. Some days… there's a physical pain in my chest that… I don't know, I just miss her."

Aubrey let silence sit between them, her heart contracting at the grief she heard just below the surface and wondered why she cared about this man when she barely knew him. When she'd first met him she'd been pretty sure he had the emotional depth of a puddle but she'd come to realize that perhaps she'd misjudged him. Seems she'd done a lot of that in her recent past.

"I wish I could've known her," she said, though she knew it would have been awkward to be face-to-face with a woman whose husband she secretly harbored illicit fantasies about. She suppressed a shudder at the hypocrisy and vowed never to admit such a thing out loud. To anyone. "She seemed like a wonderful woman."

"She was. Sometimes I wondered what she saw in me," he murmured. The power of that admission rocked her but she remained silent out of respect, knowing there was really no appropriate comeback to that statement because it was something he felt inside and no one but him could ever change that core belief. "I'm a screwup, always have been and always will be, I guess," he said bleakly.

"I don't believe that."

"You don't?" He stared at the ground, unwilling to meet her gaze until she drew his attention by lightly clasping his hand.

"No. We all screw up. It doesn't define us unless we let it."

She squeezed his hand before letting it go. He expelled a short breath and stared out toward the field. "Yeah, well, Ma always says actions speak louder than words and frankly, I've got people lining up to tell me what a jackass I've been, so what does that say?"

She smiled. "It says people care about you and

know you can do better. People rise to the level of our expectation."

"And what did people expect of you?" he asked, turning the tables on her so that she faltered.

"What do you mean?"

He looked askance at her. "I've never actually asked what brought you to Emmett's Mill."

"No, you haven't," Aubrey acknowledged with the hint of a smile. "Are you asking now?"

He paused, then nodded. "Yeah. I guess I am."

"A magazine article."

"Come again?"

"*American Photographic* featured Emmett's Mill a year ago, called it one of the top twenty places to live in the United States. I fell in love with the pictures," she said, smiling wistfully. Taking a deep breath, she added, "I also moved here to gain some clarity from the mess that my life had become."

"But why Emmett's Mill? Why not one of the other cities or towns that were featured in that article?"

She shrugged. "I don't know. It just sounded perfect. No stoplights. No nightclubs. No country clubs. Just a bunch of normal people living their lives as they saw fit instead of how others dictated because they needed to keep up appearances."

"I'd question what you consider normal," Sammy joked, then sobered. "No. I guess you're right. Emmett's Mill is that kind of place. So, what were you running from?"

"A bad relationship."

"How bad?"

She looked away and tossed her remaining pebble. "My heart was broken so I'd say it was bad enough."

"What happened?" he asked.

She shook her head. "I fell in love with this man. After a time I'd been hoping that we would get married." But now thinking of Derek brought nothing but feelings of revulsion so she wondered if maybe it had all happened for the best. "But it didn't work out so I moved on." *Way on.* "Well, it didn't end well...actually it got quite nasty. I couldn't stay in that town a moment longer."

"And that town would be..."

"Manhattan," she confessed.

"Not Vermont," he said, reminding her that she'd told a small white lie when they'd first met. She blushed and shook her head. "It's all right," he said. "There's no law that says you have to divulge personal information if you don't feel like it."

"I was embarrassed," she admitted.

"Of being from New York? I've never been there but it can't be that bad."

She chuckled. "Not of New York...just of the way I was raised. It's honestly hard to say exactly where we're from. We had houses all over the place."

He whistled low. "That's right, your family was loaded."

She made a face. "Please don't say it like that."

"It is what it is, right?"

"I guess. But we're not anymore. We're just like anyone else."

"That remains to be seen," he said cryptically and she turned to stare at him. He shrugged. "I'm just saying, you might not be as poor as you think. Sounds like Ben's got a lead on your daddy's money trail. Maybe you'll remain the Manhattan princesses."

She frowned, scooting away from him. "Why are you picking a fight with me? I can't help that I grew up differently than you. You know, I came out here because I thought you might enjoy the company but I see that's not the case so I'll leave you alone."

She slid from the fender and managed to take one step before Sammy caught her hand and pulled her back to him. She sucked in a wild breath as their chests collided softly. "What are you doing?" she asked a little breathlessly as she stared up at him, trying not to get lost in the depths of those gorgeous eyes. "This is…unseemly."

That seemed to amuse him. "Unseemly? Why, Aubrey Rose, how Victorian of you."

She scowled. "I'm just saying—"

"I know what you're saying," he cut in with a seductive growl. "And I'm just saying, I think it's cute."

Cute? Her knees went all wobbly. She opened her mouth to try and say something witty but nothing came out. Sammy took that as an invitation and claimed her lips.

His lips, cool from the brisk temperature outside, slid like silk across her own and quickly heated as he slanted his mouth to tease her tongue with his own. She clutched at him for fear of toppling over, the sensations rippling through her body and causing spirals of need spiking straight toward her nether regions that made her gasp and hold him tighter. *This was what she'd been dreaming about.*

All the hot imaginings she hadn't been able to deny in the privacy of her late-night thoughts couldn't hold a candle to the actual feel of Sammy Halvorsen pressing himself against her, plundering her mouth with the expert caress of his tongue, demanding and coaxing at the same time, until the bones in her body melted into pools of calcified goo, no longer able to handle her own weight.

He slowed and she reluctantly followed his lead until they were both forehead to forehead, breathing heavily and yearning for more but technically no longer attached at the lips. Sammy gently let go and Aubrey tried not to stumble when she was forced to stand on her own.

Aubrey couldn't find her voice so even if she'd somehow managed to put a coherent sentence together it would've come out an embarrassing croak. She was saved the effort when Sammy broke the silence first.

"Uh, well, that was unexpected," he said after a long, uncomfortable pause. He returned to his place on the rusted fender and kicked at the weeds growing at his feet. "And, uh, what did you call it? Unseemly? Yeah, that about sums it up." His cheeks pinked in spite of the nonchalant tone of his voice and Aubrey knew there was more going on in that brain than he wanted to let on.

"Sorry. That was probably way out of line. I don't know what came over me," he said.

All the giddy, love-drunk, lust-laden, girly fantasies that were floating around in her head popped like soap bubbles under a hard rain. She gave herself a sharp mental shake so that she could gather her dignity and walk away from Sammy without saying something she couldn't take back. "Me, either," she retorted. "I can't imagine what compelled you to manhandle me like that unless you thought I was Arianna again."

"C'mon now," he said, trying to make amends but not making much progress as far as she was concerned. Her feelings, not to mention her ego, were sorely bruised and she suddenly understood why his brothers had resorted to violence when dealing with him. At that moment she was not above it herself. Sammy made an unhappy sound and said, "I'm just trying to apologize for overstepping my bounds. Okay? Let's not make a mountain out of a molehill."

"Is that what this was? Nothing?" she nearly shouted, tears too close to the surface for comfort. "You're a piece of work, Samuel Halvorsen. I should've listened to my instincts and steered clear of you but I couldn't imagine leaving Ian to your deplorable parenting skills."

"Well, thank you, Miss High-and-Mighty," he returned sourly. "Are you finished? I've got better things to do than listen to you tell me what a horrible person/parent I am. Frankly, I'm over it."

Her cheeks heated but she managed to narrow her stare at him as she said, "Absolutely. So am I." Then she left him in the cold, where he belonged.

CHAPTER SEVENTEEN

SAMMY TRIED TO KEEP HIS thoughts from contaminating his family Thanksgiving dinner but each time his gaze collided with Aubrey's, her cheeks flushed and he was reminded all over again how he'd gone and screwed up. He wasn't quite sure why he'd said the things he said about her money—he could give a rat's ass that she came from a privileged upbringing—and he sure as hell didn't know why he'd kissed her like that. Regret tasted foul in his mouth for hurting her feelings and treating her so badly when all she'd done was reach out to him. He avoided looking directly at her and the reason made him want to put a hole in the wall. He'd known coming to Thanksgiving dinner was a mistake. He should've listened to his gut. But, oddly, he hadn't wanted to disappoint Aubrey. He'd seen her excitement to be included and he hadn't wanted to be the one to ruin it all. Yet, he'd gone and done just that.

"So what are your plans for Christmas, Sammy?" his mother inquired while he was ladling a second helping of potatoes onto his plate. "You know this will be Ian's first Christmas. It should be spent with family."

Sammy shrugged and dug into his potatoes. "I dunno, Ma. I'm just trying to get through Thanksgiving first."

"Let the boy enjoy his dinner, Mary," Pops instructed, which Mary promptly ignored.

"I'm just saying, Christmas is just around the corner. These things take planning."

Annabelle piped in. "Oh, that reminds me, Brandon will be home for Christmas break around the first week of December and I'd love to get all the grandkids together for a family photo before Christmas. Dean and I thought that would be a nice gift to everyone this year."

"I still don't see why Brandon couldn't make it here for Thanksgiving," Mary said with a disappointed frown. "It's not as if Berkeley is that far away."

"I know, Ma, but he wanted to spend the holiday with his girlfriend up at her folks' place in Oregon. Don't worry, I'm sure he's missing your pecan pie."

"Good." Mary nodded, returning her attention to the former conversation. "I think a photo of the grandkids is a wonderful idea."

"I agree. How sweet," Tasha said, then turned to Josh. "We have Christopher for Christmas this year, don't we?"

Josh nodded. "Yeah, Carrie is spending Christmas in Colorado this year. Some kind of time-share thing she and her new husband own."

"I love that idea, Annabelle," Tasha said with a smile.

"Do you have an idea of what you would like the children to wear?" Aubrey ventured to ask. "Like a color theme or something?"

"At first I was totally against a themed photo because I think all the kids should be able to express themselves but then I saw some photos on display at the photographer's studio and I fell in love with this one where everyone in the family wore some kind of red. It was so symbolic of unity that it brought tears to my eyes. I know…the tears were probably from my rampaging hormones but still, it was a beautiful picture."

"I think that's a wonderful idea," Aubrey murmured, shooting him a glance. "Do you have a color in mind?"

"If you say purple, I'm putting in an automatic veto," Sammy warned. "My kid ain't rocking the lavender no matter how evolved we are these days."

"No purple, I promise," Annabelle said. "But how do you feel about burgundy?"

"Isn't that a fancy word for red?" Sammy asked.

"It's a much deeper shade, very rich and sumptuous," Aubrey said a bit sharply to him, then smiled at Annabelle. "I think that would be beautiful."

Sammy leaned back and caught the bored expressions of his brothers as the women chattered about outfits and then managed to catch the approving, very self-satisfied look on his mother's face and narrowed his gaze. Oh, no, that didn't bode well. His temper flared and it took a lot of self-restraint not to let it show. But as soon as Aubrey and Annabelle started solidifying shopping plans for Ian, he jumped back into the conversation.

"That's not necessary. I'll take him shopping."

Aubrey started at Sammy's brusque manner. "It's no big deal. I'd enjoy it, actually."

"I said *no*. Thank you."

Annabelle, not quite catching the tension between them, interjected gaily, "Oh, Sammy, you have terrible taste in clothes. Just let me and Aubrey do the shopping. Besides, you hate the mall."

Sammy slammed his fist down on the table, making everyone either look up or jump. "No. He's my kid. I'll get him what he needs. I'm tired of no one listening to me." He gave his mother a pointed look that said he lumped her into that category, as well.

"There's no need to be rude," Aubrey said quietly into the uncomfortable silence that filled the room. She neatly wiped her fingers on her linen napkin and then said in a completely neutral tone that Sammy didn't buy for a second, "I heard you loud and clear." And then she rose stiffly to take her plate to the kitchen. Barbie quickly followed.

Mary stared at him. "What has gotten into you?"

"Stay out of this, Ma. You think I don't see what you've been doing? Showing up at my house, practically insisting that I hire her as my nanny. Getting all chummy with her at the Quilters Brigade, and now Thanksgiving dinner. I get it, Ma. You've all but put her in my bed in the hopes that we'll end up together, but here's the thing—I don't feel that way toward her. So quit trying to turn nothing into something." The last part was a total lie. He did feel something—too much of something, but it only served to confuse him so he'd rather just run away—but no one else needed to know that. He rose but the sound of his father's voice, stern and commanding, halted his intent to get the hell out of there.

"Boy, there will never be a time when it'll be okay to speak to your mother in that way. You are sitting at her table, eating her food, and you will treat her with the respect she deserves."

"Pops—"

"You have two options. Apologize and sit back down, or don't apologize and get the hell out until you remember the manners you were taught. That's all there is to it."

Sammy took a good look around the table and saw the faces there; his brothers wore similar disapproving expressions, while their wives simply waited anxiously to see what his decision would be. He was too far into this, he couldn't back down now. He was too angry with himself and everyone else to listen to reason. "You got it, Pops," he said, tossing his napkin down. "Thanks for the dinner. I'm outta here."

TEARS BRIMMED IN AUBREY'S EYES at the scene that just unfolded. What happened?

"We should probably go," Barbie advised quietly as they returned to the dining room where quiet, hushed conversation had ensued once Sammy and Ian were gone. Aubrey nodded, misery clotting in her throat and making it difficult to talk. Was this her fault? She knew she should've declined Mary's offer. But she'd been seduced by the image of the Halvorsen family Thanksgiving that she'd cooked up in her head and couldn't resist. She looked to her mom and said, "I'm sorry. I should've known better."

Barbie sighed. "Let's offer to help clean up and then say our thanks and goodbyes. That seems best under the circumstances."

Aubrey agreed, her heart dragging in her chest at what she knew had to come next. This time she wasn't going to try and hang on to something—or someone—who was determined to push her away. No one can say that Aubrey Rose doesn't learn from her mistakes, she thought bitterly. But the lesson still had the power to draw blood.

SAMMY WASN'T SURPRISED when Aubrey's resignation followed the next day.

"Shit," he muttered. "Way to go, ace."

If his foot could reach, he'd give himself a swift kick to the butt.

And now he had no one to watch Ian.

Swallowing his pride, he picked up the phone and dialed Annabelle.

"Hey, Annabelle, this is Sammy," he said when she answered.

"Hello, Sammy," Annabelle said. "What's up?"

He sighed. "Well, uh, it seems I'm without a nanny. Aubrey quit."

There was silence on the other end. Sammy felt the

weight of her judgment in the reservation of her tone. He wiped the sweat popping along his brow and pressed forward. "Yeah, so, I wondered if you could watch Ian for me until I find someone else to replace her."

"Um, sure, Sammy," she said. "But is there any way you could get Aubrey to come back?"

He wouldn't even know what to say to make that happen but he suspected that it wouldn't matter if he dropped to his knees and begged. "I don't know," he admitted with a sigh. "I really screwed up."

"You'd be amazed at the power of an apology," Annabelle suggested.

"I'll take that under consideration. Can you watch Ian?"

She sighed. "Yes." Then she added, "But please consider talking to Aubrey. And you know, it's none of my business—wait, no, it *is* my business because you're my family so you're just going to have to grin and bear it. You need to talk with your mom. She was really upset when you left yesterday. I think you broke her heart. And for whatever reasons she thought Aubrey would be a good fit for you and Ian, you know she had your best interests at heart."

"I know."

"Well, cut her some slack, then."

"You're right. I've been an ass. Again."

"At least you came to that realization before someone had to knock your lights out *again*."

He chuckled, but there was no heart to it. Would he ever feel right? "Annabelle, can I ask you a question?"

"Of course, Sammy."

"Do you think…" He could barely get the words out. Each time he said her name his throat closed automatically. "Do you think that Dana would've liked Aubrey?" he asked.

There was a long pause. Then she said, "Dana always kept people at arm's length because of the way we grew up. She was afraid of letting people in, afraid of people judging her. You were the first person she let see the real Dana, aside from me. I think once she got to know Aubrey, she would've loved her. But it doesn't matter if Dana would've liked her. All that matters is how you raise Ian and who you choose to help you with that task. That's what would've mattered to Dana if she'd known she wouldn't be around to raise him herself."

God, he couldn't deny the truth staring him in the face. Aubrey was probably the perfect person…just not at the right time. He had nothing to offer her. His heart still wept for his dead wife. And time was the only balm for that wound.

AUBREY FELT SHATTERED INSIDE. It was a familiar feeling, yet this time the sharp edges clattering around in there seemed to cut just a bit deeper. She shifted on the sofa, staring out the front window as rain drizzled down the pane. She wiped at a tear that managed to slip down her cheek and then amended her previous thought. This hurt way more than anything she'd felt for Derek.

She heard her mother come in and tried to hide some of her dejection but it was a losing battle.

Barbie took a seat beside her with a long sigh. "I know we haven't always been close but these last few weeks you've really shown me the caliber of person you became through no help by me, and I wish there was something I could do to make you feel better."

Aubrey smiled for her mother's benefit. "It's okay, Mom. I seem to keep putting myself into these situations so I'm the only person to blame."

"Do you want to talk about it?" Barbie asked, tucking her legs under her. "I'm a good listener."

Aubrey sighed. "I don't know. Talking about it just makes the whole mess more real."

Barbie chuckled sadly. "Funny, that's how I felt about the situation with your dad," she observed, taking a deep breath before continuing. "The thing is…I knew things were falling apart in my marriage but somehow I figured if I just kept decorating, throwing parties, being who he had wanted me to be, that things would eventually get better. They didn't. Maybe if I'd talked to someone…maybe if I'd talked to your dad… I don't know. Who knows. Maybe it wouldn't have made a difference but I'd like to think it might."

Aubrey looked at her mom. "Do you still love Dad?"

Barbie took a long moment to answer and when she did her voice was choked with tears. "I do. Damn the man but I do. I wish I didn't. Perhaps this pain would go away but I miss him." She looked quickly at Aubrey for her reaction, as if afraid Aubrey might judge her, but when she found none she said softly, "And I'd like to think somewhere in that lint-ball-size heart of his…he still loves me, too. I try not to think beyond that. It hurts too much."

Aubrey mulled over her mother's admission and felt the sadness couched within. She reached over and squeezed her mother's hand. "I'm sure he does. Perhaps when he's come to his senses…"

Barbie shook her head. "That ship has passed. You can never re-create what was lost, sweetheart. I'll cherish what we had and try to move on. Perhaps that's what you should do, too."

Aubrey leaned back, returning her stare to the rain. "Yeah. I guess. It's just hard."

I miss Ian.
And Sammy.

CHAPTER EIGHTEEN

FOR BARELY BEING ABLE TO WALK, Ian was one mobile kid, Sammy thought as he tried to wrestle the boy into one of the dozen little outfits he'd picked out in various sizes in the hopes of finding the one that fit so he could buy the sucker and get the hell out of this department store.

Ian screamed his displeasure as Sammy tried to pull a tiny shirt over his head but it got stuck on the little guy's ears instead. "Oh, crap," Sammy muttered as Ian continued to yowl and thrash his arms and legs in an attempt to get free from the garment. "I know, hold on, you're just making it worse! Hold still, Ian!"

Once he got the shirt off, Ian stopped squalling but his face was all red and tears streamed down his plump cheeks like he'd just been horsewhipped. Sammy sighed in frustration and tossed the outfits—all of which were either too big or too small—back into the cart along with Ian and wheeled back out of the changing stall. "Buddy, I know, this ain't my idea of a good time, either, trust me. But your aunt Annabelle was quite specific about me buying you something new for those damn pictures and I ain't about to let her down so c'mon, little buddy, and help a guy out."

At first Sammy thought his little pep talk worked but then Ian screwed up his face and let out a howl loud enough to bring every CPS worker within ear's reach scurrying to their location. Sammy groaned.

Until a familiar voice stopped his heart.

Aubrey.

"Samuel? Is that you?"

He turned in that direction and nearly swallowed his tongue, he was so deliriously happy to see her. His reaction shocked him. It'd only been a few weeks since the whole Thanksgiving debacle but it felt like months. He drank in her appearance until he realized he was staring perhaps a bit too greedily. He also realized he wasn't the only one who'd missed her.

Ian, the smart little bugger, twisted away from Sammy and reached straight for Aubrey.

Warmth flooded her gaze as she automatically went to oblige him, but then she checked herself with obvious effort and simply caressed his son's soft hair. Her reaction, stifled because of him, dampened his initial joy at seeing her but he didn't let it show. It was his fault she was reserved around them and he wished he could take back what he'd said to cause her to quit, but it was done, and taking it back was impossible.

"What's going on? You're...shopping?" she said, a bit dubiously, when she looked at the cart.

"I'm trying to find an outfit for Ian but I don't

actually know his size," he admitted a bit sheepishly. "But I figured it couldn't be that hard. So I've been trying all these different sizes on him and none fit."

Her mouth played with the laughter she was holding back.

"Pretty sad, huh?" he said.

She shrugged. "Why didn't you just ask Annabelle or your mom to pick something up for you? Would've saved you a bunch of trouble."

He looked away, then sighed. "I didn't want to further impose on Annabelle. She's been my nanny since... well, you left us, and, well, my mom and I aren't exactly talking yet."

"Oh," came her soft reply. "I'm sorry to hear that. I feel somewhat responsible. Would you like me to talk to her?"

He shook his head. "It's not your fault. It's mine. I'm working up the nerve to apologize. Just haven't quite made it yet." A shadow of his former self resurfaced for a moment as he added, "I'm getting close, though."

"Good," she murmured, a sweet but pained smile curving her lips. Her gaze trailed to the cart. "Would you like some help?"

God, yes. "Uh, sure. If you could spare the time..."

Her eyes lit up with genuine pleasure. "I have the time. Besides, it's not that hard once you get the hang of it." She stopped and then in a false whisper near to his ear that made his stomach muscles clench, added, "Your son wears a twelve months."

Sammy chuckled, restraining himself with great

effort from pulling her into his arms to note wryly, "The one size I didn't try. Figures."

AUBREY'S EARS HAD PRICKED at the sound of Ian's cries. At first she hadn't believed what she was hearing. The odds of her and Sammy being at the same mall in a different town at the same time were really slim but once she heard her beloved boy holler again she knew there was no mistaking that sound. It called to her heart and simply tugged her in that direction.

She saw Sammy, wearing the most adorable look of despair on his face that it made her want to smile and hug him at the same time but there was something else that nearly brought tears to her eyes. Sammy was interacting—or at least trying to—with his son. And for that she was grateful. Ian needed his father. And Sammy needed his son.

Aubrey went straight to the right size aisle and selected three outfits for Sammy's perusal.

"How do you know they'll fit?" He looked dubiously at the small outfits. "They look tiny."

Aubrey laughed. She could dress Ian in two seconds flat with her eyes closed. She knew his little body, from his chubby legs to his long torso. "They'll fit." She held one up to Ian. "See? Perfect. Now pick one."

"If you say so," he said of the sizing. "My kid has a head the size of Charlie Brown." He gestured to the one on the right with the argyle sweater vest. "I guess that one's cute. For a preppy look."

She secretly hoped that would be the one he'd pick. "Great. And—" she checked the tag "—it's on sale. Now for shoes."

"Shoes?" he complained. "What's wrong with the shoes he's wearing?"

She pursed her lips to keep from giggling. "Well, nothing for everyday stuff but Lightning McQueen tennis shoes with Velcro straps don't really match the outfit here. You need a pair of nice black dress shoes."

He looked at Ian and rolled his eyes. "Get used to it, kid. Girls and their shoes…"

At that Aubrey laughed and it felt good. Too good.

They paid and after Sammy insisted that she let him buy her a smoothie for her trouble they walked together to the parking lot.

"Well, I'm parked over there." She gestured to the south side parking lot.

"Here, we'll walk you to your car," he offered, but she declined.

"It's fine. Thank you. I hope you have a wonderful Christmas."

Sammy nodded and offered the same sentiment. He hesitated as if there were more he wanted to say and she shamelessly hung on to the hope that whatever it was had something to do with her and the terrible way they'd ended their relationship. But that hope died when he simply waved as she walked away.

The sting of her disappointment was hard to bear but she scolded herself for even going there in her mind.

They'd parted ways for a reason and though it hurt, that's the way things stood and they were unlikely to change, so she'd best get used to it. To prove her point, if only to herself, she resisted the urge to take one final look in their direction and instead focused on walking toward her own car.

CHRISTMAS CAME WITH NO WORD from Arianna, which Aubrey could tell weighed on their mother's shoulders. She didn't say anything, but Aubrey could see the dispirited slump of her shoulders when each day passed without a call or letter.

"Do you think she's okay?" Barbie finally asked.

"She's probably fine," Aubrey said, puzzling over a package that had been left by the door early this morning. It wasn't marked by postage, which meant the mailman hadn't left it. That meant someone she knew had dropped it by. That list was relatively small so she carefully opened it. When she saw what it was, tears sprang to her eyes.

It was the family photo of all the Halvorsen grandkids, with Ian in the center wearing his red argyle sweater-vest and shiny black shoes. He was so handsome. She hugged the photo to her breast even as she cautioned herself not to let it get to her too much. But it was too late. Her mother came over to see what she was making a fuss about and immediately her mouth pinched. "Now, why did he send you that? To taunt you? To remind you of how much you miss that baby?"

Aubrey started at the disapproval in her mother's voice. "Mom, I don't think that was his motivation. I ran into him at the mall in Coldwater and I helped him pick out an outfit for Ian. He's just being considerate," she explained but it didn't ease the censure in her mother's expression.

"I think you should send it back. That will send a clear message that you're not going to play his game."

Aubrey continued to clutch the beautifully framed photo to her chest, almost afraid her mother might snatch it out of her hands and toss it into the trash. The thought of sending it back made her want to throw up and she said as much. "I think this is a very thoughtful gift and I'll do no such thing."

Barbie, seeing Aubrey's hurt reaction, softened her attack. "Sweetheart, I know it's hard. But just think of how much it hurt to walk away from that baby. Another baby that's not yours. I don't see you packing around photos of those other children you cared for and you were dating their father for a time. Don't you see how this isn't healthy? I would've thought that you might've learned your lesson with Derek."

She drew back, stung, but there was a certain level of honesty in her mother's advice that she couldn't ignore. Why was she so desperate to hold on to Ian Halvorsen? She was a professional nanny, acting not so professional. She slowly straightened and reluctantly returned the photo to the box. But she wouldn't throw it away or return it. She'd just put it away with her other mementos.

Barbie smiled sadly. "You're doing what's right for you in the long run, sweetheart. I promise."

She nodded and grabbed the box to put it away. "I know," she said, but her chest ached as she said it.

BARBIE'S CHRISTMAS PRESENT came after the actual holiday but it still brought tears to her eyes.

In her hand she held the paperwork Ben Hollister had drafted and sent by courier to Aubrey's father, who had finally returned from his extended visit to the Cayman Islands with his new ladylove, Fiona, on his arm.

"I hate to say it, but men like Harold Rose are predictable. I knew he'd have to come home eventually," Ben said. "And when he did, this paperwork was waiting for him."

Barbie's hands shook as she read the contents. She frowned a few times in confusion as she read but she didn't stop to ask questions until she was finished.

"We're not broke?" she asked in a tremulous voice.

Ben smiled. "Not exactly." Then added with apologetic honesty, "But your wealth isn't as bountiful as it was. Your husband wasn't lying in that he sold the homes you owned to pay off debt but he was fudging the actual broke part. He has plenty to pay you a healthy divorce settlement, which I've outlined on page five."

Barbie returned to page five and her eyes widened. "That much?"

Ben's grin widened. "I told you I was good at finding money. You should have plenty to start fresh wherever you choose. If you invest wisely and don't spend too extravagantly, this should last you the rest of your life."

Barbie's hands fluttered and she dropped the paperwork. Aubrey knew her mother was embarrassed by such a show of nerves and so took over the conversation.

"Did you manage to talk to my father at all or was it all correspondence through my father's lawyer?" she asked.

"Actually, I did talk to your dad briefly. I'll say this for your dad that was different from the other schmucks I've chased after...he had the decency to be ashamed for what he'd done. He caved pretty easily once I was able to get him to recognize he was doing something awful to your mother. And to his daughters by proxy."

It was such a small thing but it brought tears to Aubrey's eyes. She'd had a hard time dealing with this new version of her father that she didn't know or understand. It didn't make what he'd tried to do right but at least it was something. "Thank you, Ben...for everything."

Ben laughed. "Don't thank me yet. You haven't seen my final bill," he teased.

They rose and Barbie surprised them all by clasping Ben's hand in hers to whisper in a voice choked with tears, "You're worth every penny. Bless you for coming into our lives. You've changed everything."

Ben visibly puffed up with pride and his smile reflected his pleasure at being able to help. "No problem. Glad I was able to put my evil ways to good use."

He winked and let himself out.

Barbie sank into the sofa and let out a long sigh. "It's over."

Aubrey sat beside her, a sudden sadness weighing her down. The source of that sadness surprised her but she tried to keep a stiff upper lip. "Yeah…so I guess you'll be returning to New York now."

Barbie pursed her lips as she considered her answer, and even though Aubrey saw regret, she mistook it for what it was until her mother spoke again. "No."

"No?" Aubrey repeated. "But you love New York."

"I never loved New York," Barbie corrected gently. "I enjoyed the lifestyle of New York." She took a deep breath and then looked at Aubrey. "I think…well, that is if it were all right with you, that I'd like to stay here."

"Here?" Aubrey stared incredulously, noting belatedly that she was starting to sound like a parrot. "I mean, I would love for you to stay but I just want you to be happy. Emmett's Mill is a long way from New York. The rhythm is different and no one cares about designer bags or fancy ball gowns. It's more about old-fashioned Christmas events and lunchbox raffles…and *quilting*. It's everything you always turned your nose up about."

Barbie chuckled. "I know. And I think I'm going to love it."

Aubrey grinned, hope blossoming in her chest at the thought of starting a fresh relationship with her mother after all those years of distance between them. "I'd really like that, Mom," she said. "But what about Arianna?"

Barbie's expression faltered. "I will send her some

money to get her started but I think you were right. She needs to put that degree to good use and get a job. I can't support her forever, especially if she's going to try and keep up the lifestyle she had before. If that's the life she wants…she can fund it on her own."

Aubrey whistled, then said drily, "That's going to go over well."

"We'll see. Maybe it won't be that bad."

Maybe… Aubrey didn't hold much store in that but anything was possible. Especially when it came to Arianna.

SAMMY LOOKED DOWN AT HIS SON, sleeping peacefully in his arms while the wind whistled through the shingles outside, and felt something peculiar wrap itself around his heart. The little guy had a bit of a cold so Sammy had been reluctant to put him in his crib just yet. After rubbing him down with some aromatic stuff that Annabelle had dropped off, he'd taken a bottle and dropped off almost immediately.

Sammy gazed at his son, taking in every detail, and for the first time really *saw* him.

His dark hair—almost the exact color of Dana's—curled at the ends like his.

Ians mouth was shaped like Dana's, yet when he smiled a dimple popped from his cheek—just like him.

His son was a perfect blend of the two of them. He gently touched Ian's downy cheek and marveled at the soft texture. He'd never been one to go nuts over a baby but with this kid in his arms…suddenly he got it. Was it okay to call a boy *precious?* He leaned down and pressed a gentle, yet hesitant, kiss on his son's crown. The drag on his heart was still there, but holding Ian in his arms, giving in to the love filling him with wonder, made it bearable.

Perhaps everyone else had been right all along.

His thoughts wandered to Aubrey and a different feeling followed. Smoothing a lock of hair from Ian's forehead, he wondered how to patch what he'd torn in two.

CHAPTER NINETEEN

WINTER CAME HARD TO EMMETT'S MILL, burying the town in snow and ice that killed the power to several areas for days at a time. It was one such day that Sammy arrived at Aubrey's house with a truckload of seasoned wood.

Aubrey answered the door bundled in as many layers as possible, the cold burrowing into her bones rendering her unable to care about her state of dress.

But when she saw Sammy standing there, looking fresh and yummy as a male model straight out of the Eddie Bauer winter edition catalog, Aubrey wished she'd at least been wearing something less...shapeless and ugly.

"I figured with this storm you might need a little extra wood," he said, stamping his feet on the small porch to free his boots of snow before he came in. "I brought oak and manzanita as well as some pine for kindling. Where do you want me to put it?"

"Oh, uh, there's a little covered porch off the laundry room that I've been using to store wood," she said, pointing in that direction and he didn't waste a minute. Returning to his truck, he slowly backed the

Ford until it was as close as he was going to get to the side yard and then jumped down to start unloading. Stumbling in her haste, she slipped and slid on the snowy ground until she was near to the truck. "Here, let me help," she offered, making her way gingerly to the tailgate where Sammy was tossing the wood to the sodden ground.

"Be careful," he said. "Step back until I'm done unloading."

Oh. Right. Good going city girl. She nodded and did as he requested, her insides going a bit mushy as she watched him labor in the cold. His breath plumed in frosty curls but he didn't stop until the entire truck was empty. Then he jumped down and handed her a pair of work gloves. He gave her a sidewise grin. "You said you wanted to help."

"Yes, I did," she said, slipping the gloves on. They were cold and scratchy and her fingers immediately felt stiff. She wiggled them a bit to soften the gloves, then between the two of them they had the wood stacked neatly and separated by type. She smiled at Sammy, grateful for his forethought. She hadn't realized how quickly the wood disappeared during a storm. She'd never lived in a house that didn't have central heat and air. All her little cottage had was a wood-burning stove for heat. And, once she figured out how to build a fire, she had kept that little sucker burning night and day…which was why she ran out of wood yesterday.

"I tried to call someone to buy more but apparently

you have to buy wood before winter actually gets here," Aubrey said sheepishly. "Everyone was sold out."

"Yeah. The learning curve here is a little steep at times," he said with a chuckle, the sound sending little sparks of something sizzling through her body. "So…"

"Come in for something hot?" she blurted out, then blushed. "I mean, let me make you a cup of coffee or something. I have tea, too. Or hot cider?"

He smiled, clearly enjoying her rambling, though she wanted to fall through the porch at that moment. Why couldn't she, just once, be the cool, sophisticated lady that's always in control of the situation? "I'd love some," he said.

"Great. I mean, good. Right. This way." *Shut up.*

Stamping their feet free of snow and mud, they entered the house through the side yard. They both kicked off their boots in the laundry room, and then Aubrey disappeared into the kitchen while Sammy made himself comfortable on the sofa. "Decaf or fully leaded?" she hollered.

"Decaf."

"Instant or brewed?"

"Whatever you have ready and available."

Her cheeks burned as she wondered what he'd say if she offered herself next. She selected the instant and then rethought that decision and returned it to the shelf. Who offered instant decaf to their guests? That was like offering beans and franks at a dinner party. Tacky. So instead, she pulled out her coffeemaker and started making a fresh pot.

Within minutes, the coffee was ready and she brought a steaming mug to him. Then she stopped. "I forgot to ask how you like your coffee. Sweet? With cream?"

"Black is fine," he assured her. He eyed her speculatively. "Everything okay? You seem jumpy. I could go if I'm making you uncomfortable. I know things haven't been so smooth between us."

"No," she rushed to say, almost so desperate to have him stay that her dignity screeched in protest but she didn't care. She calmed her nerves and risked a smile. "No...I'd love to visit if you wouldn't mind."

He looked relieved, as if he'd been hiding his own jitters behind that million-dollar smile. She handed him the mug and took a seat beside him, then second-guessed herself and wondered if she should've sat in the chair opposite him. Her indecision must've read on her face, for he reached out and tenderly cupped her chin as he said, "It's fine. Really."

She smiled, the touch of his hand igniting those tiny sparks that had jumped to life earlier, causing a small fire in her body. "I guess we're in foreign territory," she said.

He surprised her when he shook his head. "Not for me," he said gently.

"What do you mean?" she asked, almost painfully breathless.

He let go and leaned back. "What would you say if I told you that I've been looking for a suitable excuse for days to come and see you?"

"I'd say...why?"

He shook his head. "Since you've been gone I haven't been able to get you out of my head. At first I thought it was because of Ian but then I realized it was because of me. I missed having you around."

That statement doused the fire. "Oh?" she said stiffly. He missed having her around? Like a comfy chair or lamp? "Well, with time I'm sure you'd get over it."

He chuckled quietly and his expression softened as he watched her. "Oh, I tried. Believe me, I tried." Then he went from amused to dangerous in a heartbeat and Aubrey felt her mouth go dry. He looked…*hungry*. And not for a cheeseburger. "But when I stopped fighting it I realized I wanted you. Plain and simple. What do you say about that?"

She swallowed hard, feeling as if all the moisture in her body had suddenly been routed south. She couldn't even find the words. "I…I…" she stuttered, trying for some kind of rational, mature response but failed completely so she just said, "Okay."

That was all he needed. Before Aubrey saw it coming or knew what happened, she was flat on her back and Sammy was stretched above her, pressing her into the sofa with all that delicious bulk of his that called to that ultrafeminine side of her. And then she tipped her head up and he claimed her mouth.

Thick swirls of desire ebbed and flowed, bathing her body in wonderful liquid warmth that quickly heated her blood to the point that she was ready to shuck her clothes if he so much as said the word. It was heady and dangerous and so exactly what she needed after all these months of wanting but not being able to touch.

She wound her legs around his torso and jerked him closer to her so that she could feel that thick length of him riding against her and she moaned into his mouth.

As they devoured each other, Aubrey was nearly lost to all reason until Sammy broke the kiss and stared down at her with lust-glazed eyes to ask hoarsely, "Is your mother home?" By the way he asked, she knew he was hoping they were alone.

She shook her head wildly, eager to return to what they'd been doing. "She's actually with your mother on some Quilters Brigade errand," she answered, just as breathlessly. "I would've been gone, too, but I had a headache."

His mouth turned up in an adorably devilish smile. "A headache, huh? Lucky me."

No, she thought, lucky me. And then demanded his mouth again.

HE TRULY HADN'T COME OVER hoping to end up on Aubrey's couch, all but attacking her like a horny teenager who didn't know what else to do, but Sammy wasn't one to complain when opportunity presented itself.

When she'd opened that door she'd looked really frumpy. The shapeless bulk of her many layers left a lot to the imagination, but honestly, he hadn't really seen all that. His eyes had feasted on her face. He'd come to

love that face. There. He admitted it. A weight fell off
him. It had snuck up on him and then slapped him when
she'd quit. He'd fought it tooth and nail but he recognized the feeling, even if it was a little different from
what he'd shared with Dana. It'd just taken him a while
to figure out how to tell Aubrey.

Suddenly, he felt her hands pushing against his chest
and she made a small sound of protest. "Is there something wrong?" he asked, worried.

She took a moment to catch her breath but then she
said, "Not that I don't enjoy what's going on, because
I do, but I have to wonder what's going on? I mean, we
haven't actually been around each other for months and
it's not like we've been chatting on the phone this whole
time…. I just don't understand and you have to know
that I'm not the kind of woman who could be one of
your—" she blushed in an adorable fashion then lifted
her chin and finished with "—one-night stands."

He nodded and slowly climbed off her with great
regret before helping her to sit up. "I don't want a one-
night stand with you, Aubrey," he said, then leaned back
against the sofa, feeling much like he was getting ready
to bare his soul because maybe that's what he needed
to do. "I have feelings for you, Aubrey. I don't know
where it will go but I want the chance to find out. It's
been over a year since Dana died. I didn't think I'd ever
be ready to go there again with someone else but then
you came along at the worst time ever for me and
I had to fight every day the way I was starting to feel.

It wasn't right. I felt like I was betraying Dana," he admitted with a heavy sigh but it felt good to get it out there. He looked at her. "But I realized—too late—that Dana would never begrudge me happiness. She just wasn't that kind of person."

Aubrey's eyes watered at that admission but she shook her head. "Sammy...you don't know me well enough to love me. There're things about me that..."

"Are you a murderer? A felon? A thief?" he interrupted with a half smile until she blurted out what had been the deal-breaker for Derek.

"I can't have children."

Sammy stopped and stared, not quite understanding at first. Then his brain caught the import of her words and he frowned. "You can't have kids?" he asked. "Why not?"

Aubrey wiped at her tears and she seemed to shrink before his eyes, something he'd never seen her do, not even when he'd been a complete jerk to her. But that one question had caused her to wilt like a dehydrated plant in the Sahara desert.

"Does it matter?" she asked, pained. "I just can't."

When she realized he wasn't going to be satisfied with that answer, she compressed her mouth as if she were going to clam up but then started to explain in a shamed voice that cut him to the heart for her pain.

"You see...I've had a pretty bad track record with guys," she said. "Before Derek...there was my college boyfriend, Chuck. When we broke up I didn't realize he had given me the gift that kept on giving. I got really sick and landed in the hospital. I had developed pelvic inflammatory disease." At Sammy's look of confusion, she explained. "PID is caused—most often and as was in my case—by an undiagnosed case of…chlamydia. By the time the doctors discovered what was going on, the disease had destroyed my reproductive system. The doctors—and I've been to many—have all said the same thing. I'll likely never get pregnant."

It took a moment to digest that information but it was a moment too long. Aubrey rose and put distance between them. "Don't worry. It's too much for most men," she said, crossing her arms. "I understand."

He rose, intent on protesting, but there was a niggling of doubt. Did he want more children? He'd never really given it much thought. Actually, with how difficult his start with Ian had been, he hadn't even considered more kids but to have that choice taken from him…it threw him a little. She read that hesitation and walked away. "Thank you for the wood. If you don't mind I will mail you a check."

Sammy started to go after her but he realized he didn't know what to say. He'd come hoping to start something, but really, he might've just squashed any possibility between them.

CHAPTER TWENTY

SAMMY FOUND HIMSELF AT DANA'S grave. It was the last place he swore he'd ever willingly visit but somehow before he'd even realized where he was going, he was there.

The Emmett's Mill cemetery had countless of his kin buried there. The Halvorsen roots went way back, all the way to the town's beginning, and Sammy had no doubt that when his time came, his bones would rest there, as well.

The cemetery itself was nothing to look at. Dry, brittle weeds managed to poke through the frozen ground in various spots, clustered around headstones that tottered from age and the passage of time without a caretaker to straighten them. Some were so old they simply crumbled to dust.

The elevation was lower here and only saw snow a few times a year, so he found himself kneeling on the cold hard ground before Dana's grave, staring at the marble stone that he'd willingly paid a fortune for.

For a long moment he simply stared, reading each word on her stone slowly as if it was already burned into his brain.

Dana Collins Halvorsen
Born May 15, 1979
Died February 12, 2008
Wife, mother, best friend
My heart goes with you.

He'd chosen those words because he'd known his heart was going into the ground with his wife. He'd felt cold, empty and desolate inside. The void had kept growing, sucking everything up like a black hole eating whole solar systems until he was a walking pile of nothing.

Then there was Aubrey. Smart, sweet, giving, yet strong and resilient—she was everything he didn't want to be attracted to.

Tracing the letters carved into the marble, he felt the words start tumbling out—painful and wrenching, but once they started, he was helpless to stop them.

"I never thought I'd say this, never wanted to even *think* that I'd say this, but, baby, the truth is I've fallen for a woman who loves our son more than I ever thought possible for someone who didn't give birth to him. If you could see her with Ian…I think you'd be good with her raising him. She's kind and generous…" He stopped short, tears blinding him. Hell, what was he doing out here? He wiped at his eyes and nose, his heart cracking. "Dana…baby…I miss you so much. I'm half the man I was without you, that ain't no lie, but Aubrey manages to make me feel alive again and as much as I miss you,

I can't have you back so I have to make a decision. Either I love her with everything I got or I hold on to the memory of what we had and slowly die from the pain of losing you. And I can't do that. Ian needs me. I've been a shitty father up until recently and Aubrey helped me see that. God, I'm so sorry but I blamed—" the tears streamed down his face at his confession "—Ian for your death and that wasn't fair but I wasn't thinking right. I think I'm finally getting my head on straight because when I look at him…I don't see a kid who took away the one person in my life that I loved the most…I see our son. I see a little boy who looks just like his mama and I know a piece of you will always be with me. But I have to let go. I have to."

And then the floodgates opened and he sobbed like a baby. He cried as he couldn't at her funeral. Great big racking sobs that were ugly and true, the loss bone-deep and sorrowful. He cried like a husband who is saying the final goodbye to his wife; a husband who bears the burden of knowing he'd never again feel his wife's soft touch; a husband who will never again delight in his wife's laughter. Sammy Halvorsen wept the tears of a man ready to accept that a chapter had closed and a new one had to begin.

And when he finally walked away from that cemetery—stiff, frozen and emotionally spent—Sammy knew the answer to Aubrey's question and he couldn't wait to set things straight.

But first he had a mess to clean up.

AUBREY WAS TRYING TO MAKE the best of things. She'd even applied to the school district for a position as a counselor in an attempt to put her degree to good use, but a part of her was dragging, hoping every knock at the door or phone call was Sammy, coming or calling to apologize. But the days stretched on and on with no such luck.

And Barbie was no help, either. She was back in society mode, even if it was modified to fit Emmett's Mill's particular pace and she was having a ball running around with Mary Halvorsen as they formed committees, gossiped and bickered.

Although she didn't begrudge her mother new friends, it stung a little that Barbie and Mary had become tight friends—odd couple that they were—because Aubrey had to bite her tongue in half to keep from asking after Ian, and, of course, Sammy, whenever Barbie spent the day with Mary.

Each night she went to bed and gave a mental kiss to Ian as he stared back at her from the picture frame, smiling and waving as if he knew she was watching him, wondering if he was eating well enough, and if Sammy knew what size to buy when it came time to purchase new clothes.

She fretted over things that were out of her control, and frankly, she really had no business to care about.

And when fatigue finally pulled at her eyelids, her last thought was of Sammy. His touch, his smile, the way he pushed her buttons in all the right ways, and how much she missed being a part of his everyday life.

It was a funny thing to realize you were in love with someone when half the time you had spent together had been wasted on being adversarial. When she'd fallen for Derek he had been the man with the plan, the stock alpha guy. He'd wined and dined her, flattered her endlessly and played the part of the gentleman until the point where she admitted to him that she was incapable of carrying a child. She hadn't thought it would matter much as Derek had already had Nikki and Violet. But suddenly she had lost her appeal and he had quickly moved on, cutting off all ties as if she'd been contagious.

God, that had hurt. Damaged her in a very real way, but it was nothing compared to the daily rending of her heart that she felt being apart from Sammy and Ian.

Somehow they had burrowed in deep and nothing could get them out. That didn't bode well for her, she thought morosely.

What rotten luck she had with men. Perhaps she'd have better luck as a lesbian. If she'd had any scrap left of her sense of humor the dark comment might've cracked a smile from her lips, but as it was she simply grabbed the throw pillow and covered her face with it so she could scream.

And then the doorbell rang.

Tossing the pillow, she slowly got to her feet and went to the door, grumbling as she went, fully expecting to see the poor, hapless UPS man standing there apprehensively with a package in his hand. She was ashamed to admit that she'd snapped at him more than once when she'd gotten her hopes up that it was someone else only to find Frank holding that little gizmo for her signature.

She opened the door and gasped. Now, she'd envisioned this little scenario a million times, but when it happened and Sammy was actually standing there her mind went embarrassingly blank and all she could do was stare. "What are you doing here?" she finally said when she found her voice.

"I've come to answer your question," he said, watching her with a grave expression.

She furrowed her brow. "What question?" she asked, trying to cull her memory for the slightest inkling what the heck he was talking about. Why couldn't he just sweep her into his arms as he was supposed to? She pursed her lips and crossed her arms. "I don't recall any question that needed answering."

He pushed forward with a grin, forcing her to move back or he'd crush her slippered toes. "Hey," she exclaimed with a scowl. "Watch it."

"My apologies," he said, closing the door behind him. "Now, as I was saying…"

"Yeah?" she said suspiciously. "What were you saying?"

He held up a finger. "First, this." And then he pulled her to him and laid a lip-lock on her that curled those same toes and caused a moan to burst free from her mouth even as he plundered it with abandon. Her knees knocked together as the strength disappeared from her limbs and she had to cling to him just so she didn't go straight down on her rear. He slowed the kiss and she almost whimpered with disappointment. He smiled at her reaction, pleased. "Now that you're in a better frame of mind," he teased softly, and her scowl returned but not with the same ferocity as earlier. He sobered as he caressed her face. "The answer to the question you didn't actually ask but was written all over your face is this—I'm in love with you...not your uterus."

She blushed and started to pull away, but he wouldn't let her. "So you can't have kids. Big deal."

"But you're still young. You might want a sibling for Ian," she protested, tears welling in her eyes. "It's not fair to either of you."

He chuckled. "Let me be the judge of that. And besides, I've already decided that if down the road you and I want to expand the family, there are plenty of kids out there who need a good home. Josh and Tasha announced they're going to adopt a child from Punta Gorda—that's where Tasha was stationed when she worked for the Peace Corps a few years back. I say let's adopt. I'm open to it if you are. What do you say?"

She opened her mouth as if to voice more doubt, but then her eyes filled with warmth and joy and Sammy knew his answer had been the right one.

"I say..." Her eyes twinkled and she bloomed with radiant energy that was nearly so bright it hurt to look at her. She curled her arms around him and purred. "I'm open to whatever you have in mind, Sammy Halvorsen. But for the time being…we've got some catching up to do."

And then she pulled him to the bedroom.

EPILOGUE

AUBREY'S HEART WAS FULL to bursting. To say she was happy seemed so trivial a description to capture the feelings coursing through her at that moment.

With two-year-old Ian in her lap and Sammy at her right, they sat in the pew along with the rest of the assorted friends and family as Tasha and Josh christened their child, four-month-old Michael Atl Halvorsen, and officially welcomed him into their family.

Her eyes watered at the love flowing between Josh and Tasha as the priest sprinkled water on the infant's fuzzy, black-haired head. He twisted in Tasha's arms as if he were trying to discern where the drops of moisture were coming from, but he didn't cry or fuss.

Afterward everyone gathered at Josh and Tasha's house for a barbecue to celebrate the grand occasion of Michael's christening as well as the final signing of the paperwork for his adoption from the Belize City orphanage. Aubrey glanced down at the dazzling ring gracing her finger, a gift and pledge from Sammy given only days prior.

She was going to marry him.

As she watched the comings and goings, listened to the laughter and reveled in the comfort of such a close-knit family she knew she'd finally found a place she could call home—and a man she couldn't wait to spend the rest of her life with.

For Aubrey, there was no greater—more unexpected—gift in the world and she wasn't above savoring it for the rest of her life.

And that's exactly what she planned to do.

* * * * *

Celebrate 60 years of pure reading pleasure
with Harlequin®!
Just in time for the holidays,
Silhouette Special Edition®
is proud to present
New York Times *bestselling author*
Kathleen Eagle's
ONE COWBOY, ONE CHRISTMAS

Rodeo rider Zach Beaudry was a travelin' man—
until he broke down in middle-of-nowhere South
Dakota during a deep freeze. That's when an angel
came to his rescue....

"Don't die on me. Come on, Zel. You know how much I love you, girl. You're all I've got. Don't do this to me here. Not *now*."

But Zelda had quit on him, and Zach Beaudry had no one to blame but himself. He'd taken his sweet time hitting the road, and then miscalculated a shortcut. For all he knew he was a hundred miles from gas. But even if they were sitting next to a pump, the ten dollars he had in his pocket wouldn't get him out of South Dakota, which was not where he wanted to be right now. Not even his beloved pickup truck, Zelda, could get him much of anywhere on fumes. He was sitting out in the cold in the middle of nowhere. And getting colder.

He shifted the pickup into Neutral and pulled hard on the steering wheel, using the downhill slope to get her off the blacktop and into the roadside grass, where she shuddered to a standstill. He stroked the padded dash. "You'll be safe here."

But Zach would not. It was getting dark, and it was already too damn cold for his cowboy ass. Zach's battered body was a barometer, and he was feeling

South Dakota, big-time. He'd have given his right arm to be climbing into a hotel hot tub instead of a brutal blast of north wind. The right was his free arm anyway. Damn thing had lost altitude, touched some part of the bull and caused him a scoreless ride last time out.

It wasn't scoring him a ride this night, either. A carload of teenagers whizzed by, topping off the insult by laying on the horn as they passed him. It was at least twenty minutes before another vehicle came along. He stepped out and waved both arms this time, damn near getting himself killed. Whatever happened to *do unto others?* In places like this, decent people didn't leave each other stranded in the cold.

His face was feeling stiff, and he figured he'd better start walking before his toes went numb. He struck out for a distant yard light, the only sign of human habitation in sight. He couldn't tell how distant, but he knew he'd be hurting by the time he got there, and he was counting on some kindly old man to be answering the door. No shame among the lame.

It wasn't like Zach was fresh off the operating table—it had been a few months since his last round of repairs—but he hadn't given himself enough time. He'd lopped a couple of weeks off the near end of the doc's estimated recovery time, rigged up a brace, done some heavy-duty taping and climbed onto another bull. Hung in there for five seconds—four seconds past feeling the pop in his hip and three seconds short of the buzzer.

He could still feel the pain shooting down his leg with

every step. Only this time he had to pick the damn thing up, swing it forward and drop it down again on his own.

Pride be damned, he just hoped *somebody* would be answering the door at the end of the road. The light in the front window was a good sign.

The four steps to the covered porch might as well have been four hundred, and he was looking to climb them with a lead weight chained to his left leg. His eyes were just as screwed up as his hip. Big black spots danced around with tiny red flashers, and he couldn't tell what was real and what wasn't. He stumbled over some shrubbery, steadied himself on the porch railing and peered between vertical slats.

There in the front window stood a spruce tree with a silver star affixed to the top. Zach was pretty sure the red sparks were all in his head, but the white lights twinkling by the hundreds throughout the huge tree, those were real. He wasn't too sure about the woman hanging the shiny balls. Most of her hair was caught up on her head and fastened in a curly clump, but the light captured by the escaped bits crowned her with a golden halo. Her face was a soft shadow, her body a willowy silhouette beneath a long white gown. If this was where the mind ran off to when cold started shutting down the rest of the body, then Zach's final worldly thought was, *This ain't such a bad way to go.*

If she would just turn to the window, he could die looking into the eyes of a Christmas angel.

* * * * *

*Could this woman from Zach's past
get the lonesome cowboy to come in
from the cold...for good?
Look for
ONE COWBOY, ONE CHRISTMAS
by Kathleen Eagle.
Available December 2009 from
Silhouette Special Edition®.*

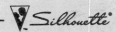

SPECIAL EDITION

**FROM *NEW YORK TIMES* AND *USA TODAY*
BESTSELLING AUTHOR**

KATHLEEN EAGLE

ONE COWBOY,
One Christmas

When bull rider Zach Beaudry appeared
out of thin air on Ann Drexler's ranch,
she thought she was seeing a ghost of
Christmas past. And though Zach had
no memory of their night of passion years
ago, they were about to share a future
he would never forget.

*Available December 2009
wherever books are sold.*

SSE65493

Visit Silhouette Books at www.eHarlequin.com

Silhouette® *Desire*

New York Times Bestselling Author

SUSAN MALLERY

HIGH-POWERED, HOT-BLOODED

Innocently caught up in a corporate scandal, schoolteacher Annie McCoy has no choice but to take the tempting deal offered by ruthless CEO Duncan Patrick. Six passionate months later, Annie realizes Duncan will move on, with or without her. Now all she has to do is convince him she is the one he really wants!

Available December 2009 wherever you buy books.

ALWAYS POWERFUL, PASSIONATE AND PROVOCATIVE

Visit Silhouette Books at www.eHarlequin.com

REQUEST YOUR FREE BOOKS!

2 FREE NOVELS PLUS 2 FREE GIFTS!

HARLEQUIN®

Super Romance®

Exciting, emotional, unexpected!

YES! Please send me 2 FREE Harlequin® Superromance® novels and my 2 FREE gifts (gifts are worth about $10). After receiving them, if I don't wish to receive any more books, I can return the shipping statement marked "cancel." If I don't cancel, I will receive 6 brand-new novels every month and be billed just $4.69 per book in the U.S. or $5.24 per book in Canada. That's a savings of close to 15% off the cover price! It's quite a bargain! Shipping and handling is just 50¢ per book*. I understand that accepting the 2 free books and gifts places me under no obligation to buy anything. I can always return a shipment and cancel at any time. Even if I never buy another book from Harlequin, the two free books and gifts are mine to keep forever.

135 HDN EYLG   336 HDN EYLS

Name	(PLEASE PRINT)	
Address		Apt. #
City	State/Prov.	Zip/Postal Code

Signature (if under 18, a parent or guardian must sign)

Mail to the **Harlequin Reader Service:**
IN U.S.A.: P.O. Box 1867, Buffalo, NY 14240-1867
IN CANADA: P.O. Box 609, Fort Erie, Ontario L2A 5X3

Not valid to current subscribers of Harlequin Superromance books.

**Are you a current subscriber of Harlequin Superromance books
and want to receive the larger-print edition?
Call 1-800-873-8635 today!**

* Terms and prices subject to change without notice. Prices do not include applicable taxes. Sales tax applicable in N.Y. Canadian residents will be charged applicable provincial taxes and GST. Offer not valid in Quebec. This offer is limited to one order per household. All orders subject to approval. Credit or debit balances in a customer's account(s) may be offset by any other outstanding balance owed by or to the customer. Please allow 4 to 6 weeks for delivery. Offer available while quantities last.

Your Privacy: Harlequin is committed to protecting your privacy. Our Privacy Policy is available online at www.eHarlequin.com or upon request from the Reader Service. From time to time we make our lists of customers available to reputable third parties who may have a product or service of interest to you. If you would prefer we not share your name and address, please check here. ☐

HSR09R

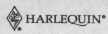

INTRIGUE

FIRST NIGHT
BY
DEBRA WEBB

To prove his innocence, talented artist
Brandon Thomas is in a race against time.
Caught up in a murder investigation,
he enlists Colby agent Merrilee Walters
to help catch the true killer. If they can survive
the first night, their growing attraction
may have a chance, as well.

Available in December wherever books are sold.

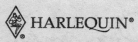

HARLEQUIN®

A Cowboy Christmas
MARIN THOMAS

2 stories in 1!

The holidays are a rough time for widower
Logan Taylor and single dad Fletcher McFadden—
neither hunky cowboy has been lucky in love.
But Christmas is the season of miracles! Logan
meets his match in "A Christmas Baby," while
Fletcher gets a second chance at love in "Marry
Me, Cowboy." This year both cowboys are on
Santa's Nice list!

*Available December
wherever books are sold.*

"LOVE, HOME & HAPPINESS"

www.eHarlequin.com

HAR75292

HARLEQUIN® Super Romance®

COMING NEXT MONTH

Available December 8, 2009

#1602 A MOTHER'S SECRET • Janice Kay Johnson
The Diamond Legacy
Bad enough that Daniel Kane's mother harbored a secret about his heritage. Now Rebecca Ballard is doing the same thing! Forget her—Daniel's son is going to know his father. But it's a hell of a time to realize he still cares for Rebecca....

#1603 PLAN B: BOYFRIEND • Ellen Hartman
Hometown U.S.A.
Sarah Finley has always done what's expected of her and her ruddy husband leaves anyway! God help Charlie McNulty, the only guy in her ex's firm brave enough to help when she loses it...and pins her sights on him.

#1604 BABY UNDER THE MISTLETOE • Jamie Sobrato
A Little Secret
All eco-friendly Soleil Freeman and military guy West Morgan have in common is that fling they had...until she discovers she's pregnant. Now these two—who couldn't be more different—have to find a way to raise a child...together.

#1605 A SMALL-TOWN REUNION • Terry McLaughlin
Built to Last
Devlin Chandler is here to make peace with his past. And that brings him to Addie Sutton. Though they'd once missed acting on their connection, now neither will let that moment slip away. But when secrets are revealed, can Addie and Dev make it last?

#1606 THEN COMES BABY • Helen Brenna
An Island to Remember
Jamis Quinn wants to be left alone. Then Natalie Steeger moves in next door, and he's drawn to the vivacious woman. When she becomes pregnant, Jamis is forced to face the world again. But he's not sure he's up to it....

#1607 THE CHRISTMAS PRESENT • Tracy Wolff
Uptown lawyer Vivian Wentworth is not the defense attorney Rafael Cardoza wants for his wrongfully accused client. But her dedication to justice surprises Rafael... almost as much as his attraction to her.